Raton - Text copyright © Emmy Ellis 2024/25
Cover Art by Emmy Ellis @ studioenp.com © 2024

All Rights Reserved

Raton is a work of fiction. All characters, places, and events are from the author's imagination. Any resemblance to persons, living or dead, events or places is purely coincidental.

The author respectfully recognises the use of any and all trademarks.

With the exception of quotes used in reviews, this book may not be reproduced or used in whole or in part by any means existing without written permission from the author.

Warning: The unauthorised reproduction or distribution of this copyrighted work is illegal. No part of this book may be scanned, uploaded, or distributed via the Internet or any other means, electronic or print, without the author's written permission. The author does not give permission for any part of this book to be used in AI.

Published by Five Pyramids Press, Suite 1a 34 West Street,
Retford, England, DN22 6ES
ISBN: 9798312725254

RATON

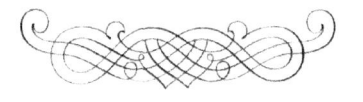

Emmy Ellis

Chapter One

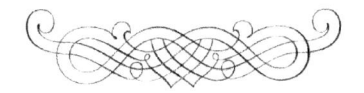

Time waited for no man, so the saying went. Tommy Coda wasn't exactly in the mood to employ patience anyway, not when he had a shedload of stuff to sell from the back of the French Café. His stupid ex, Leanora Archambeau, had finished with him before he could put his plan into action, so he'd had to send round a couple of heavies to manipulate her into doing what he wanted without her realising it was him who pulled the strings.

He leaned on the railings beside the Thames and stared out over the water. A sharp slice of wind slapped him in the side of the face, so bloody cold, further waking him up from the nap he'd had this afternoon. It was supposed to only be short and sweet, a resting of his eyes, but he'd ended up kipping for two sodding hours, waking groggy and disorientated.

It was now that no-man's land of time between lunch and dinner, so he'd left his swanky house and walked the short way along the street to the chippy. He'd bought sausage and chips then strode over the road to stand here and eat them. A gull had been that rude in flying up to him and stealing a chip right out of the packet—brazen, like a shitload of others around here, thinking they could take whatever they wanted without asking. Just the other day a neighbour had had their bike stolen. Tommy had moved to this street because it was supposed to be upmarket, but it seemed thieves couldn't care less about ruining an area's reputation.

Food gone, he popped the packet in the bin and opened a can of cola. He should have made tea in his flask really, it would have heated him up nicely, but you didn't become rich by squandering your money, so he'd brought the shop-brand can out with him rather than buy one at an exorbitant price in the chippy. What was it they wanted, two-fifty for it? Fuck that.

Leanora had a different view on that kind of thing. She said life was for living and money was for spending, and what was the point in having it if it was going stale in a bank account when you could be having the time of your life? He should have known from that comment alone that they weren't destined to stay together. Incompatible. They'd have rowed.

He missed shagging her, though. If she was any indication of what French women were like in the sack then he'd never fuck a British one again—but he'd have to, as there wasn't exactly an abundance of ladies from Lille around here. He adjusted the crotch of his trousers, a bit uncomfortable down there as it happened. Christ, she really must have got to him if he was getting excited at just the thought of her. What was she, some kind of witch who'd cast a spell? Ironic, when it was him who thought *he'd* been the spellcaster, luring her in with his charm online, getting her to believe he wanted to spend the rest of his life with her, kids, a dog, the lot. Maybe, had he been a few years older, that might have been on the cards, but he was too young for all that commitment crap. He'd loved her, though, as much as he could love someone. Mainly, he'd needed her to buy the café so he had somewhere to store and sell his shit, a front that no one would take any notice of unless they fancied a cup of tea and a slice of cake.

He'd pushed her too far, too quickly. Oh, and he hadn't got the proper measure of her before she'd walked out on him—he'd been so full of himself that he'd thought he'd controlled her when he'd done no such thing. He'd tried to discipline her too early, bullied her too early, and she'd surprised him by caring more about herself than she had him or their relationship. She'd spouted some nonsense about self-worth and then left him, going to live in the flat above the café which had been vacant the whole time she'd been living with him. Perhaps she'd been the clever one all along, not renting the flat out to someone else. Maybe, even though she'd told him she had no family or close friends in France, she *had* spoken to someone who'd warned her not to put all of her eggs in one basket.

It annoyed the fuck out of him that he'd completely underestimated her.

He'd do better with the next one.

For now he'd continue to influence her from behind the scenes, using the two heavies he was paying to do the intimidation, leaving him looking innocent. Who knew, she might run to him for protection—better that than The Brothers, he supposed. The heavies, also twins, were called Joel and Noel but went by the nickname of the Unidenticals because they weren't a carbon copy of each other.

Tommy knew what they looked like beneath their ever-present balaclavas, he'd known them for years, but many others wouldn't have a clue. They'd been warned to keep Tommy's name out of things if The Brothers caught up with them. Tommy had paid them well to keep their gobs shut, even if it meant they took a kicking in the process. The thing that bothered him, though, was that there was only so much people were prepared to take before they broke. The Wilkes pair were infinitely scarier than Tommy. If push came to shove, the Unidenticals might cave under pressure.

It was a risk Tommy had to take. He had no one else he felt comfortable enough to do business with.

He glanced at the time on his phone. Noel and Joel would be here in a minute, likely with their balaclavas on despite the masks drawing attention. They rarely went anywhere without some form of covering on their faces, and many a time they disguised their voices, masters at different accents. Half the shit they got up to was attributed to the real twins—people getting beaten up or warned away from certain areas. It was a good scam they had going, basically imitating the leaders of Cardigan, but if those leaders ever found out…

Tommy turned in a circle to check the vicinity. The Unidenticals' car prowled by slowly, Noel likely trying to find a parking space. He found one farther along the street outside the chippy, slotting it into place and then getting out to scan over the road in Tommy's direction. In normal circumstances a wave would be appropriate, a mate greeting his mates, but Tommy nodded instead, keeping it professional.

He lowered his gaze but could still see them. Faces obscured, hands in pockets, their strides an almost perfect match for those of The Brothers, they headed towards him. If Tommy didn't know better he'd swear blind they *were* the proper twins, but their clothing gave them away. No grey suits, white shirts, and red ties. Mind you, that outfit was for official business. Surely George and Greg must turn to black tracksuits like these two from time to time, but Tommy had yet to see it.

He turned away from them to face the water, bracing his elbows on the railing. An Unidentical stood either side of him, but with their faces obscured, he had no clue who was who. He'd be able to tell once they spoke. Joel had a rougher edge to his tone.

"What's the state of play?" Tommy asked—he required a weekly face-to-face update on how Leanora was behaving.

"I'm worried she's going to fuck this up." Noel, to the left, gripped the top bar of the railing, the black wool of his gloves squeaking.

Tommy's stomach rolled over, a knot of anxiety forming. "Why would she play up when she hasn't before?"

"Didn't you hear what happened last night?" Joel asked.

Tommy shook his head. The customer hadn't said a dickey bird. *And neither have these two.* "Do I want to know?"

Noel tutted. "Seeing as this is your operation, I should fucking well think so."

"Is it bad?"

"Bad enough."

"Then why didn't either of you tell me about it sooner?"

"Because we went round there and sorted it out, then talked her off the ledge."

Unease slithered inside Tommy. *That bitch…* "What kind of ledge?"

"The 'telling the twins' kind."

"Shit." Tommy took a deep breath and watched the jostling water, wishing Leanora floundered in there, unable to swim, the current ready to take her beneath the surface and keep her there forever, out of his fucking face.

He snatched himself from the visual to concentrate on the present. On the one hand he paid these two to take care of business, but on the other, if Leanora was on the verge of contacting George and Greg, this was a different kettle of fish, wasn't it? He should be having a right old mare at them for not telling him about it immediately. He'd make a firm decision on that in a minute once he'd heard what had happened. No point flipping his lid unless it was really necessary.

"What went on, then?" he asked.

"She refused to let the buyer in," Joel said.

Tommy's anger immediately fired up. Why couldn't people just do as they were fucking told? "All she has to do is let them in, take the money, hand over the goods, and send them on their way. For that she gets to keep breathing. I honestly don't see what her problem is."

"Maybe you need to give her a sweetener. She's been doing this for you for free and probably realises she's missing out on a good few readies. She's got used to us turning up in the café kitchen willy-nilly to scare her, and regardless of the balaclavas, I don't think she's bothered by us anymore. We keep saying we'll hurt her but never do."

"Then shit her up next time you go round there, cut her face with a knife or something so she knows you mean business. Remind her of the first time you introduced yourself to her, how frightened she was."

Joel took a packet of cigarettes out of his pocket and lit one of them. "Nah, I don't think scaring her is the way to go anymore. She's shrewd. She's a businesswoman. You'll need to make her an offer she can't refuse."

"If I give her a slice of the pie, that's less for us three." Tommy hadn't discussed the intricacies of money with the Unidenticals, and he wasn't about to admit that giving Leanora some wouldn't make much of a dent, but he had to at least put on a show of protesting, otherwise these two might up their fee.

"Don't try to mug us off," Noel said. "You're raking it in. Giving her five hundred a week isn't going to make much difference, and anyway, if she's being paid, we can film her taking the money, letting her *know* she's being filmed, then you've got her over a barrel when it comes to the next time she's thinking of tiptoeing up to that ledge. Then you save money with us, because we wouldn't have to go round there so often to remind her of why she needs to store the gear at her café."

"Does that mean you don't actually need this gig?" Tommy had no one else to monitor this shit—no one he trusted anyway—and the idea of the Unidenticals not needing his cash sent a bolt of shock through him. What was it his mother had once said? *Don't get complacent, son...*

Joel flicked his partially smoked cigarette into the water. "This job is just one in a long line for us. Going round and scaring her every so often is child's play, and dropping the gear off to her isn't exactly stimulating. If we lose this gig, another will come along and take its place. We've already made the big money by going round there the first time. These small top-ups you're paying us, it's just beer money."

Tommy scoffed. "I hardly think a grand every time you visit her is beer money. That's five hundred pounds each to say a few menacing words, drop off some stuff, and then fuck off again." He thought about the ridiculous 'menu' of prices the Unidenticals had, so not only did he pay them a grand for the scaring aspect, there were also prices for other things, like taking customers to the café in the middle of the night.

"Which reminds me," Noel said, "us being phoned by your customer because Leanora wouldn't hand over the goods meant we'd been pulled away from a surveillance job, which, as you can imagine, was a bit of a pest because the job title is a big clue in what we were meant to be doing."

"Surveilling," Tommy said.

"Yep, except we weren't exactly doing that, were we? Instead, we were getting in your ex-bird's face and telling her we'd slice her fucking cheeks off if she didn't play ball, all this in front of the customer."

Why weren't they already there? Why did the customer have to ring them? I'm paying them for this shit… Does he even realise he's slipped up? "How were things left?"

"The customer was happy in the end, if that's what you mean, but don't be surprised if he doesn't want to do business with you again."

They're not doing their job properly. "Are you actually meeting the customers, blindfolding them, and taking them to the back of the café?" Tommy asked.

"We give you itemised bills…" Joel lit another cigarette.

"Doesn't mean you're doing the work, though. You could be sending the customers round there on their own—I mean, you've already admitted it."

"No we didn't."

"You did, you said you were called to the café by the customer—when you should have already been there with them."

Tommy glanced across at Joel, who, going by the narrowing of his eyes inside the balaclava holes, he had a fuck-off big frown going on.

"I'll pretend not to be offended," Joel said, "but if you expect us to babysit these customers after the first time we take them to the café, when they can make their own way there happily enough…"

"I do if I'm paying you for it."

"Fair enough, but like I said, this job is one in a long line and something else will come along to take its place. We don't *need* your money."

Tommy panicked. He needed them—even if they *were* diddling him. "Ignore me. I was having a moment, but the reason for the blindfold is so the customers don't see where the drugs are stored—otherwise, they could go round to the café and steal it all."

"Hmm," Noel said. "Didn't think of that."

"Do you think I need to go around and see Leanora?"

"We've got her covered, but think about giving her some money, eh? You need the visual proof of her taking it from my hand. Insurance."

Tommy nodded. "Next time there's a problem in the middle of the night where she's having a bit of a wobble, please let me know and I'll come round and deal with her myself." He'd wear his clown mask and change his voice, and she'd rue the day she'd ever started thinking she had some say in this scam. "And if you're not going to take customers to the café blindfolded after the first time, I'm going to have to employ someone who will. I can't have people knowing where the gear is stored."

"We'll resume normal duties," Joel said. "At least one of us will anyway."

Tommy produced an envelope and passed it to Noel. The Unidenticals each patted him on the back then walked away. Tommy didn't watch them go. He stared over to the other side of the river until the sound of their car engine faded in the distance. Then he returned home, taking one of the burners out of its hiding place, reciting

Leanora's phone number over and over in his mind.

Fuck it. He was going to ring her. She needed to be put back in her place.

Chapter Two

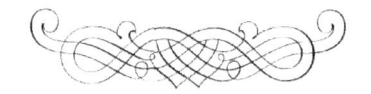

Amidst the chatter and hubbub of her café, Leanora struggled to breathe. The sound of the automated voice in her ear brought on a rash of goosebumps. Ever since those men in balaclavas had laid out the rules, she'd been a nervous wreck; getting a full night's sleep was a joke, and as for eating…not much passed her lips without her wanting to be sick.

She couldn't do this here, in front of other people. She didn't want anyone to know she hid a dark secret. While a lot of her customers had welcomed her with open arms, many of them curious as to why she'd come to this "shithole" instead of staying in France, she didn't want to do anything to jeopardise their friendliness.

"I wouldn't advise that you ignore me," the caller said.

"What do you want?" she whispered, rushing out the back, through the kitchen and into her little office, leaving her assistant, Sally, to watch the café.

"I hear you refused to let the latest nighttime client in."

Legs giving way, she lowered herself onto the chair behind the desk, her whole body trembling. This must be the boss of the men in the balaclavas.

"I don't know what's in those packages inside the boxes, but it can't be legal." *It's drugs, you know it is.* Except she'd never seen it, as such. She took packets, already in carrier bags, out of the boxes for the customer. "I don't want anything to do with it. It's not right that you're forcing me to do whatever you want. I'm protected by The Brothers…"

"See, that's where you've got a little bit mixed up. You seem to think you've got a choice in the matter. What makes you think going to the twins will save you?"

"They'll keep me safe."

"Did it ever cross your mind that you're doing this for them?"

On the day she'd first met the balaclava men, she'd collected a tray of things from one of the tables and taken it out the back. When she'd returned to the café, it had been empty apart from a man in a balaclava, pointing a shotgun at her. He must have told all of her customers to get out. He'd ordered her to close the blinds. She'd thought about running via the kitchen to get away, but he'd informed her another man was in there with Sally. She recalled the conversation she'd had, saying to the man on the line:

"One of the men told me I wasn't allowed to snitch to the twins, *that's* how I know it isn't them."

"That could've been a big fat lie," the caller said. "A bluff."

Why was the voice automated? So she didn't recognise it?

"I know you, don't I?" she said.

Going by the sharp intake of breath, she'd hit the nail on the head.

"Who the fuck are you?" she snarled, a whoosh of braveness flooding her body. "A customer in my café? Some hardman you are, if you can't even speak to me using your real voice."

"You'd better watch what you're saying," he said. "Or I might have to send one of my men round to teach you a lesson."

Her stomach flipped over, but she wasn't going to be frightened, not anymore. She was sick of this. "You're a coward if you couldn't even come here and threaten me yourself. You sent two men with their faces covered, one of them with a gun. Go on, send them now, and they might just find there's someone waiting for them when they get here."

"Are you suggesting the twins will be in your café?"

"What do *you* think?"

She ended the call, her hands shaking. God, what had she done? She'd be better off getting hold of The Brothers now, but what about her part in this mess? Yes, she'd been forced into it, and she'd been frightened to death, especially by the man with the shotgun, but she'd stored God knew what. Would George and Greg expect her to take accountability on that score? After all, what she should have done was gone along with whatever she'd been told during that first meeting and then phoned the twins straight after. They could have set something up so they'd have been here for when the first customer had arrived in the middle of the night.

And it would have all been over.

Although would it? It sounded like this was bigger than the balaclava men, considering someone else had just rung her. What if there was a whole network out there? What if all the nighttime customers were in on it? To begin with, they'd only ever arrived with the balaclava men, and they'd been blindfolded, so she'd felt a measure of relief that they didn't know who she was or where they were. But then things had changed. The customers had turned up by themselves, so she'd immediately felt vulnerable because they'd seen her face and knew damn well where the goods were being stored. That's why she'd refused to serve that customer last night. She'd spoken to him through the locked back door, telling him to go away, then he'd got hold of those thugs who'd arrived and threatened her.

What if telling the twins made it worse? It wasn't like they'd send someone here to look after her, was it? She wasn't anyone important. She wasn't a true resident of the Cardigan Estate, she was French for a start, so maybe they'd remind her of that and ask her how she could be so rude as to expect them to treat her the same as people who'd been born and bred here.

She recalled what George had said when they'd first introduced themselves: "French, you say? What the bloody hell have you come here for? Not that it's any of our business. So long as you pay the protection money and behave yourself, everything will be fine. We don't care where you've come from if you play by Cardigan rules."

So that dissolved that worry, they were fine with her being an outsider, but what they wouldn't be fine with was her basically colluding with East End residents to store and help sell whatever was in those boxes.

Her phone rang again, and she jumped, the same number on the screen from last time. Whoever it was hadn't even bothered to withhold it so was likely using a pay-as-you-go mobile. She pressed the answer button and waited. Heavy breathing filtered down the line, and she couldn't stand to keep quiet any longer.

"I've phoned them," she lied. "I've told them I need to talk to them about something, so it's in your best interests to come and collect the boxes before they get here. They'll be here within the hour."

"You fucking little bitch. You're going to regret that."

He cut the call, and a ripple of fear went through her. She'd probably made the biggest mistake of her life, but if the caller had any common sense, he'd get the stuff picked up and leave her alone.

She popped her phone in her pocket and marched out into the café, a surge of adrenaline pushing her forward. Behind the counter, she spoke to Sally and asked her to stay out the front for the next hour, then she went to the storeroom beside her office, which she kept locked. She took the keys from her pocket and opened the door, stepping inside to stare at the boxes. Only four of them remained from the latest drop-off, so it wouldn't take long for her to drag them into the back yard.

She eyed her own storage section along one wall and took out a pair of gloves, disposable ones her sandwich lad used when prepping every morning. She slipped them on, not wanting her fingerprints to be transferred, and gripped hold of two corners of one of the boxes. She bent her knees, ready to lift, but the contents were too heavy. She'd suspected drugs were inside, likely tightly packed bricks of cocaine or something, but to actually have her suspicions confirmed by this weight… Or could it be weapons?

Either way, she wanted them out of her café.

She turned to the bright-yellow dolly standing in the corner, the one she used when the food deliveries arrived. She loaded the box onto it and took it down the ramp and into the yard. She left it there on the rain-drenched patio area, uncaring whether the cardboard got soggy, returning inside to collect the other boxes. Once they were all dumped in the yard, she went in and locked the door, going to stand at her office window behind the thick net curtains. She wanted to see who came to collect, whether it was the balaclava men or the person on the phone—if he was even a third player. It pissed her off that she didn't know if he was one of the original two just messing with her head.

Her phone rang in her pocket, and she jumped again, annoyed with herself for allowing it to frighten her. But that was normal, wasn't it? Most people would be scared to have random men forcing them to do things they didn't want to do.

She swiped to answer. "What?"

"It's Martin."

Shit, she hadn't checked the screen, and now the twins' money collector wanted to talk to her. What about? Were protection payments going up? Or had the twins secretly been watching her café and had noticed things going on out the back in the dark?

"Is everything okay?" she asked—*merde*, her voice sounded unsteady.

"Yes, I'm just letting you know I won't be around to collect any money until tomorrow. I've got a bit behind and I didn't want you to worry that you'd missed me dropping in."

"Thank you for letting me know."

"See you tomorrow then."

It was on the tip of her tongue to ask him to advise her regarding a meet-up with the twins, but he'd severed the connection. She popped her phone in her pocket and stood to the side of the office window, prepared to stand there for however long it took for someone to come and collect those boxes.

Ten minutes later, the gate opened and someone in a clown mask entered the yard. Jolted by the creepiness of it, she stared at the face—it looked rubber, had a round red nose, pure-white skin, and a painted pink smile. The top appeared to have a frizzy orange wig sewn to it.

Whoever this was struggled to take the boxes out of the yard by hand, pushing them along with a foot so they shunted through the gateway and out into the street beyond. Once all four had been removed, the clown stared at the office window. Leanora wasn't visible, she was sure of that, but the person was likely asking themselves if she watched them.

The clown raised two fingers in the shape of a gun and mimed pulling the trigger. Then he ran through the gateway, the orange hair wobbling behind him, and slammed the gate shut. She wasn't stupid enough to go out there at the moment to lock the gate, but she was desperate to do just that. Instead, she went up to her flat to look down at the yard and the street, again hiding behind a net curtain. The clown had trouble lifting a box and, glancing left and right, slit open the top. He tossed the bricks inside the van one by one, and she took pictures with her phone, zooming in on the number plate so she had that, too.

She was now armed with evidence of who this person was. Unless the van was stolen or the plate was fake. The clown got into the van and drove off, leaving the empty boxes on the pavement. Leanora rushed downstairs and out of the yard, bringing the boxes back in — the clown hadn't had gloves on, so the twins might be able to get fingerprints off the cardboard.

She took them inside, back into the storeroom, locked the door, and typed a WhatsApp message.

LEANORA: THERE'S SOMETHING WE NEED TO TALK ABOUT.

Chapter Three

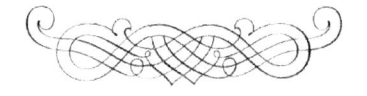

LEANORA ARCHAMBEAU: *Hi, I'm new to the group and currently live in Lille, France. I have a dream to open a café in London, England. I wondered whether anyone knew of any properties coming up either for sale or for lease. I have looked on*

the internet, but none of the places are quite what I have in mind.

BEEFY_BOY: *What *do* you have in mind?*

LEANORA ARCHAMBEAU: *Something small, intimate rather than a big place. Ideally in a high street so people can stop by for a coffee while they're shopping.*

TOMMYCODA: *What sort of café is it, because people around here aren't going to want snails or frogs' legs.*

LEANORA ARCHAMBEAU: *Very funny. Baguettes, cakes, pastries, that sort of thing.*

TOMMYCODA: *There's one that's just come up for sale in the East End. If you don't mind me private messaging you, I'll pop over the link to it.*

LEANORA ARCHAMBEAU: *Thank you, that's very kind.*

Chapter Four

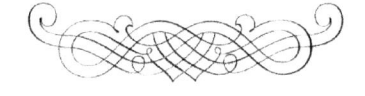

Tommy sat in his living room with the curtains open and stared out at the night-blackened Thames with its jagged, reflected lines of light on the surface from the buildings opposite. The tranquil scene usually calmed him, but not at the moment. Rage swirled inside him, even now, hours after the events that had sent him all but apoplectic. How fucking *dare* she speak to him like that, despite all those threats from the Unidenticals to keep her in line. And what about how he'd had to rush out and collect those pissing drugs? She'd said the twins were going to be there within the hour, yet he'd gone there anyway, regardless of the risk. The drugs meant more to him than his safety, clearly. Or the money they generated did.

What he didn't understand was why she'd told him to collect. Why hadn't she kept the drugs as proof they existed? Was it that abhorrent to her she'd just wanted them off her property?

What a monumental fuck-up. He should have chosen a new location and a new person after she'd left him, then this wouldn't have happened, but Tommy being Tommy, he'd known best, and because he hadn't wanted all those weeks of online chatting to go to waste, he'd continued with his original plan.

What was Leanora doing now? Telling the twins exactly what had gone on? Thank God she wasn't aware it was Tommy behind all of this, because you could bet they'd be knocking at his door soon if she had. The idea of her laughing at him—of all three of them doing it—sent heat to his cheeks. He'd been bullied as a little kid at school, so imagining how they could be taking the piss out of him right now, even though they only knew him as a man in a clown mask, well, it didn't sit right.

He thought about how it could have gone if they'd turned up at the café while he'd been there. Yes, he'd had a mask on, but that didn't mean they couldn't have ripped it off to reveal who he was—he couldn't imagine them doing anything else. In the whole time he'd lived in the East End, he'd stayed under their radar, so they likely didn't even know who he was by name or sight, but going by the rumours about them, it wouldn't take long for them to find out. He'd be sought out, caught, and tortured, information spilling out of him as quickly as blood from any holes they poked into him with knives or corkscrews or…

He let out a groan of frustration and, to be completely truthful, a squeak of fear. He was a hardman in his own right, but he was nowhere near the twins' level. Their ruthlessness…he'd never be able to match it.

He sipped his tea. Shuddered. He didn't like to admit he'd got antsy in that yard, expecting

George or Greg to come storming out of the café, catching him red-handed. His face had been so hot beneath the mask, getting him worked up even further, and when the boxes had been too heavy, fucking hell, he'd wanted to scream. It had felt like the whole world was conspiring against him.

Now he had a shit ton of drugs stored in his van and a couple of customers due to go to the café just after midnight to buy some of it. He messaged the Unidenticals to let them know he'd have to think about a new location, because the café was now out of bounds. He didn't bother telling them why.

His work phone rang, Noel's name on the screen.

"For fuck's sake," Tommy griped. He should ignore it. He wasn't in any fit state to talk. Regardless, he answered the call. "I told you I needed a minute to have a think, yet you rang me anyway."

Noel tutted. "Well, you're going to have to think pretty sharpish then, because tonight's customers aren't going to want to be seen buying out in the open—like you selling on a street corner."

"I'm way past that," Tommy said, annoyed Noel could even *think* he'd stoop to that level these days, but if he didn't find a place to sell from, he might well have to resort to hanging around outside in the dark.

"What's happened regarding the café?" Noel said.

Might have known he'd ask.

Tommy didn't want to talk about it. Everything seemed to crowd in on him at once, a smack-smack-smack of issues parading through his mind, and anxiety coiled at the top of his stomach. He was going to have to face at least one part of what was upsetting him, though, and even by him thinking that, his gut clenched again. He'd get a fucking ulcer at this rate.

"I phoned the silly bitch to warn her not to fuck you about, and she didn't even sound fazed, like she'd grown a massive pair. She said she'd got hold of the twins. Gave me an hour to go and collect the drugs. I suppose I ought to be grateful for that."

"She could have made that offer for a reason. She might have been filming you…"

Tommy hadn't thought of that, and it irritated him, so he barked, "I'm not a div, I put a mask on."

"Where's the gear now?"

Tommy stared out at his van. "It's safe for the moment but not overnight, so I need a new location as soon as possible."

"What about our lock-up? It'll cost you to rent floor space, but the offer's there if you want it—until you find another location."

That wasn't a bad shout. Their lock-up was better than his van, and if the shit hit the fan, at least the drugs would be miles away from him. When he'd collected them earlier, he'd doctored his number plate by using black tape to change a couple of letters and numbers, so he'd covered his arse there, too.

You can bet they'll keep using the blindfold method now it's their *property being used to collect from. They'll actually do what I pay them for.*

"When can I drop it round?" Tommy asked.

"We'll nip over there now, seeing as it's dark."

"How much rent are we talking?"

"Fifty quid a day." A pause. "Per box."

Fuck me sideways, they're always so quick to take the mick.

Tommy totted it up in his head. It was more than he wanted to pay, especially when a new delivery arrived and there'd be a shedload of boxes, but it wasn't as if he had much choice, was it? "It's a deal. Fair warning, though, I've got another job for you."

"Don't tell me, you want the French bint sorted."

"Yeah."

"Thought so."

"But I don't want you killing her. I just want her picked up. We'll chat about that soon."

Tommy ended the call. He went back out the front and crouched to add some more black tape to his number plate; he'd removed the last lot when he'd arrived home earlier. Satisfied it was sufficiently different to what it had been before, he set off in the direction of the row of lock-ups. He drew up in the forecourt, parking outside the one in the middle. The Unidenticals' car wasn't there yet, so he folded his arms and waited.

A few minutes later, the beam of headlights flashed in his rearview mirror, temporarily blinding him. He glanced in the wing mirror to his right, checking Noel and Joel had arrived and that it wasn't some geezer who rented one of the other units. Relieved when the Unidenticals got out of their car, both in balaclavas, Tommy lurched out of his van.

"So you didn't offer her any money to continue storing your stuff, then?" Joel asked.

"Very funny," Tommy said. "The conversation went downhill pretty fucking rapidly, and she had the cheek to put the phone down on me." He moved to the back of the van and unlocked it.

Noel and Joel stared inside.

"Fucking Nora," Noel said. "Are you telling us we've got to carry each brick into the fucking lock-up one by one? What happened to the boxes?"

Joel sloped off.

Tommy's face flamed hot. "They were too heavy for me to lift on my own so I had to empty them."

Noel eyed Tommy's hands. "Please tell me you had gloves on."

Balls. I wasn't thinking, too arsey… "Err, no."

Noel tutted. "So each brick's going to have to be wiped over." He gestured forward. "On you go, get in the back of the van."

Tommy gawped at him, appalled he was going to have to do as he was told when usually it was him who dished out the orders. But he'd fucked up good and proper, there was no denying that, so he got in the van and fished out an old rag from his toolbox. He swiped it over the packaging of a brick and then passed said brick to Noel. He handed it to Joel who placed it in a large bag usually used by builders' merchants for delivering sand or pebbles. He must have gone and got it from either the lock-up or their vehicle.

"Hold up," Tommy said. "If we fill that bag, it's going to be too heavy for us to get it indoors."

"It's sitting on our trolley," Noel said.

Tommy frowned at it, swearing it hadn't been there before. How come he wasn't noticing shit like that lately? Was he losing his marbles? "I didn't hear either of you pushing that along."

Noel shrugged. "We've perfected the art of being silent."

That sounded ominous somehow, and it gave Tommy the willies and thoughts of the Unidenticals creeping up on him in the dark, waylaying him before he had a chance to react.

Nah, they wouldn't do that to him.

Would they?

The coke was now stored in cardboard boxes with pictures on the outside giving the impression they contained fruit-scented candles, which they did, but only one row on top of the bricks. If anyone other than Noel or Joel took it upon themselves to look at the contents, not that anyone would, they'd see nothing untoward. However the coke was stored, Tommy didn't care so long as it was away from his property or van. Now his fingerprints had been wiped off every block, if this lock-up got raided he was safe as houses evidence wise. If it came to the Unidenticals grassing him up for being the actual owner of the drugs, he believed they'd do anything to save their own skin. He'd do the same if the tables were turned. They were all loyal to each other but only up to a point.

In the top-left corner stood a kitchen cupboard floor unit. On top, a kettle beside a large flagon of drinking water. Noel went over there and filled the kettle to halfway, then bent to open one of the cupboards to take out an old ice cream tub containing teabags, individual servings of milk in little pots, and sugar sachets that looked to have been pilfered from McDonald's and KFC. The same went for the wooden stirring sticks. He took three polystyrene cups from a stack of them in the cupboard, a bottle of bleach beside them.

That might be needed later for any blood when Leanora dies.

Tommy had always known, on some level, that if someone got in is way and needed to die, he'd arrange to get rid of them, he just hadn't anticipated it actually happening by *his* hand. Or that he'd even *want* to be the one doing it, yet he must do on some level, because he'd watched scenarios flickering through his mind as he'd tried to get to sleep of a night, seeing himself as this competent killer, efficient and brilliant. In reality, he was more of a wheeler and dealer, he'd never had to resort to violence other than a few well-chosen words designed to shit people up, all while his face had been shielded. He bought large quantities of drugs from a man much savvier and scarier than himself, always paid him up front, and he sold those quantities to club owners, street-corner plebs, pub landlords, you name it. All he wanted to do was make a packet then fuck off into the sunset, preferably abroad—undeniably a cliché, but he'd be the last one laughing.

"So what's the plan?" Joel asked. "With the French bird?"

"Give me a sec." Tommy hastily cobbled together a plan in his mind, flipped through it again, then laid it all out in the open. "It'll work, won't it?"

Noel put teabags in the cups. "Yes, providing the Wilkes twins have been and gone and don't take her with them. We're going to have to go over to the café and nose around first before we even think about getting inside. That will cost you more."

Tommy resisted rolling his eyes. Didn't they get home *important* this was? "I don't care what it costs, I want her brought here. I'll kill her while you keep watch outside, then I'll take her off and dump her somewhere."

"Where?"

"I still need to think about that."

The kettle clicked off, steam curling from the spout, and Noel poured water into the cups then stabbed at the teabags with the stirring sticks. "You two can put your own milk and sugar in yours." He collected what he needed and took his tea to a faded green patio table tucked in the top-right corner, hidden behind a tower of cardboard boxes containing God knew what.

Once they were all settled around the table, they discussed the ins and outs of what was going to happen, even the pitfalls, and Tommy realised how good it was to have someone to bounce ideas off of. Noel and Joel were lucky they had each other. Maybe Tommy ought to get an advisor, but who could it be? The two people he trusted, and even then only to a certain level, were the Unidenticals. He couldn't let his mum know that his career as a car salesman was a complete front for being a drug pusher. There wasn't even a brother or sister he could turn to, and because of the nature of his business, other than Noel and Joel, he'd never confided in any other mates or acquaintances.

The least amount of people who knew what he did behind the scenes the better.

"So you're going to wait here for us while we got and get her?" Noel asked.

Tommy nodded. "It's probably best I don't go to the café with you. You two are used to working together, and having me there, I expect I'll get in your way. I'd be like a stick in a bike wheel—fucking annoying."

What he hadn't said, and didn't plan to, was that he didn't want to expose himself to any danger. The twins could be at the café when they arrived, and Tommy didn't plan for them to catch him creeping inside. Going there earlier with the added pressure of them possibly turning up any second had bothered him more than he'd thought it would.

It worried him that he had to rely on Noel and Joel, or he'd *chosen* to rely on them, but they were far better at this kind of thing than he was. They'd always been the ones he'd asked to do the grunt work. He was more than a tad uneasy, though, at the prospect of this going wrong.

"With her dead," he said, "I'll sleep a lot easier, so let's get this job over and done with as quickly as possible, then normal business can be resumed."

"Or the *new* normal business," Joel said, "with the drugs now being stored here."

"Do you know what the pisser is?" Tommy asked. "That café. She's got no family, no mates. There's no one for it to be left to, so the government will end up getting it."

"Maybe, because she's from France, the French government will get it."

Tommy seethed. "I don't know how these things work, but it's annoying however it plays out. She split up with me, waltzing off, before I got the chance to persuade her to put my name on her business documents."

"You should have cut all ties once she'd fucked off," Noel said.

Tommy scowled. "Don't rub it in, I'm well aware of that."

"I'd never have had you down as a killer. You're not the type."

"Nope, but I'm not forking out the amount of money you two will want to do it, and I can't see you offering me a freebie, can you?"

"Not with something this big, no."

They drank their tea, and it reminded Tommy of the old days when they'd first got started, the Unidenticals with their business run from their parents' garden shed, Tommy working from his mum's garage where he'd hidden the drugs inside an old wicker laundry bin that used to stand on the landing when he was a kid—a kid who'd imagined a snake lived inside it.

If only things had stayed that simple.

He'd welcome a snake over the imminent murder any day.

Chapter Five

George and Greg laughed at something Moon had said. The older leader had been ill, but you wouldn't know it to look at him. Thanks to the wonders of modern medicine and backhanders at a private clinic to ensure he got the best care, he was living his life full of purpose. That didn't mean he was running the Moon

Estate all guns blazing, his right-hand men did that for him, something they'd been doing while he'd been ill or, as George and Greg had been led to believe, he'd been taking a step back to live a better life with Debbie, his missus.

George had been worried about her. She'd once been one of Ron Cardigan's Treacles—women he'd had on the side, women like George and Greg's mother who'd had no choice but to have sex with him. A few of them had got pregnant, but the only child Ron had acknowledged openly was the daughter he'd had with his wife. Debbie had become more than a Treacle, though. Yes, Ron was an utter bastard in many, many respects, but Debbie had assured them he'd loved her. And now here she was, with another older man, another estate leader, and it didn't take a rocket scientist to work out she clearly needed a father figure to care for her. She appeared a lot happier than she had when they'd last seen her. She'd lost that hollow look that had haunted her face lately, as if now, at last, she'd accepted she wasn't going to lose the man she loved to Mr Grim Reaper—again.

She must have been worried she'd be known as a black widow.

With the fire crackling in the grate and their coffee cups depleted, George had a rare moment of experiencing what many other people must—calmness, contentment. It was foreign to him, to sit like this in Moon's house or even at home, where just for a brief snatch of time, he had no worries on his mind. Then his brain piped up and ruined it all. It seemed something was up if the message from that bird who ran the French Café was anything to go by. After he'd read it, he'd convinced himself the talk she wanted was nothing more than her having a gripe about Martin needing to pick the protection money up tomorrow instead of today—not exactly anything that needed their attention at the minute. He hadn't responded yet and only planned to once they were back on the road.

Which came sooner than he'd thought.

"You two can fuck off now," Moon said. "You've outstayed your welcome."

George preferred the bloke's bluntness so wasn't upset. He rose, happy enough to sod off, but put on an offended act anyway. "Charming. Remind me next time you're at death's door not to give a shit, and I certainly won't be bringing you grapes and chocolates."

"Those are appreciated, but you needn't have. We'll catch up some other time. Have dinner at the Taj." Moon didn't bother to get up, instead letting Debbie do the honours of showing them out.

On the front doorstep, a chill wind snapping at George's neck, he did up the buttons of his suit jacket and wished he'd brought a proper coat with him. "This weather could freeze the fucking balls off a brass monkey."

"Which is why I'm not going to stand here with the door open," Debbie said.

"Fuck me, you're as rude as him. There isn't anything we needed to discuss anyway, so bog off back indoors."

Everything that had needed to be said since Moon had taken ill had been done over WhatsApp with Debbie, George and Greg being reassuring during her lowest moments. He'd been tempted to tell her that if she insisted on shacking up with older men she had to expect them to get poorly from time to time, but that would have been cruel and unnecessary, and he was learning to be a bit more empathetic towards people. That didn't mean it was coming easy, but at least he was giving it a go.

"We'll leave you to it then," Greg said.

George was tempted to kiss Debbie on the cheek but thought better of it. She'd likely slap his in return for drawing out emotions she didn't want to face now Moon was better. Like how it could have all gone so wrong and this visit would be for an entirely different reason—planning his funeral.

"See ya," he said and got in the passenger seat of their BMW.

Once Greg had driven out onto the main road, George asked, "What did you think? Were they covering anything up or were they telling the truth that he's right as rain?"

"You could always pop to the clinic and lean on them a bit to tell you what the actual score is."

"And risk Moon sending Alien and Brickhouse to teach me a lesson for poking into his private medical records? No thanks."

"Scared of them, are you?"

"Am I fuck, but two against one, not good odds."

"You'd have me on your side. And we have guns." Greg smiled. "By the way, what was that message you got on the work phone?"

George sniffed. "From that French tart in the café. She said there was something we needed to talk about. I'll message her back now."

GG: We'll visit your café tomorrow for a chat. Ten a.m.

"There, sorted." George's stomach rumbled. "Moon talking about the Taj has made me hungry."

"I take it that was a hint for me to drive there."

"Of course it fucking was."

Greg tutted and changed direction, leaving George to his thoughts. Irritated that the café owner hadn't got back to him yet, and telling himself he hadn't exactly responded to her immediately either so ought to cut her some slack, he reached forward for a lemon sherbet from the glove box. Greg signalled he wouldn't mind one, so George popped it in his brother's mouth and then added one to his own.

George crunched on his sweet then swallowed it. Checked the phone again.

GG: Did you get that message I just sent?

Still no response.

Fuck her.

He chuckled and planned out his dinner menu in his head.

Chapter Six

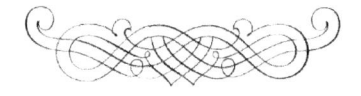

Leonora had been unable to read the messages on her phone because those big balaclava men were at the café again. Fear roiled inside her. She deserved to be in this position for being so damn stupid. Because she'd messaged the twins, she'd thought it was *them* knocking on the back door so had gone to answer it—without checking through the office window first. She'd regretted it instantly, especially because it also could have been the man in the clown mask returning, but she'd been so desperate for help and to spill her side of the story that she hadn't been thinking straight.

You weren't thinking at all.

Now, with the blinds of the café drawn down and a shotgun once again pointing in her direction, Leanora couldn't remember the question she'd just been asked. All sense of reality had disappeared, leaving her in a fog of *unreality*, where everything had turned on its head and she had no control whatsoever. Alice falling down the rabbit hole. She wished she could close her eyes and wake up somewhere else, or wake up here without those men staring at her, their eyes so creepy surrounded by the black wool of their masks.

She wished she could rewind time. She'd never have come to London.

"Are you fucking deaf?" the man with the shotgun asked.

She thought of him as Number One; he generally did all the talking, the threatening, ever since she'd met the pair of them. Number Two was more of an afterthought, although, she conceded, he was no less dangerous. He could probably hurt her with his hands rather than using a weapon, so maybe he was the one she really needed to watch out for—he didn't need a gun in order to freak her out. He had, on occasion, hurt her with his words alone. He'd called her some nasty things and smiled while he'd done it.

She shook her head, terror blanking it. She had to force herself to *think*, to get the words out, words they'd want to hear. Ones that wouldn't get her in any trouble. Or more trouble than she was already in.

Her mind flashed back to when they'd burst in via the back, one rushing upstairs, the other taking her by the arm as he'd kicked the door shut and forced her to go with him around the downstairs rooms. Even in her panicked and distressed state it had been obvious the pair of them were checking she was alone. How long had they been outside? Had they watched to see whether The Brothers had come and gone? Or were they that sure of themselves they'd taken the chance that if The Brothers had been there, they'd have shot them?

"Have The Brothers been?" Number One asked when they congregated in the café itself.

"What?"

"The twins, you told them about the operation. They were coming to see you. Have they already been?"

"No."

"You'd better not be lying."

"I'm not!"

"So they could be here at any time?"

"Yes."

"Then we'll just have to stay on our guard, won't we. I've got no problem with taking those two out. If you've got a problem with it, then you'd better do as you're told, when you're told, so we can get out of here before they arrive."

"Why the fuck are you just standing there, staring?"

She jumped at Number One barking at her. "Sorry… I'm nervous. W-what did you s-say? Before?"

He sighed. "I said you need to go and pack a bag."

Pack a bag. Pack a bag. Her stomach churned, but there was a spark of something inside her, maybe optimism. If she had to pack a bag, did that mean she was only being kidnapped? *Only. As if that isn't bad enough.* "W…why?"

"Because I said so."

Going by the look on his face, she shouldn't have questioned him; she was getting on his nerves, or maybe his worry about The Brothers turning up was making him testy. He flapped the gun about, his finger curling around the trigger, although the business end wasn't aimed at her, thankfully.

But it might be if she kept saying stupid things.

"What are you going to do to me?" she asked, fear forging a hot path through her gut then sending her skin cold. Her legs weakened, as did her hands. They shook uncontrollably, and she willed them to stop, for her mind to stop showing her the terrifying scenario of her brain being spattered all over the wall.

He jerked the gun about again. "Listen to me, you irritating Frog bitch."

She flinched at the insult—Tommy had called her that once or twice. It must be a slur the English used more frequently than she'd thought.

"How many times have we come here and told you that *we* ask the questions and *you* answer them?" he snapped. "How many times have we said that what *you* want doesn't matter? Isn't it obvious what we're going to do to you? Are you that dumb you can't work it out, or are you burying your head in the sand?"

"You said I needed a bag, so does that mean you're not going to kill me?"

"No, it means you're going to text your washing-up girl and your sandwich lad to say you're going back to France—and packing a bag will make them think you're telling the truth if they ever come here and see clothes missing."

She struggled to work out whether that had answered her question. Because he'd said no, it implied she was going to be killed. On the other hand, he'd mentioned France. In other, less dangerous circumstances, understanding his meaning would have been easy, but for the life of her she just couldn't do it. "How long for?"

"There's no need to tell them a timescale. Stop stalling by asking me shit."

She should have known he'd work out what she was up to. Because her message tone had gone off, she told herself it was the twins responding, and she'd gone so far as to imagine what they'd said: that they'd be here soon for a chat. If she could waste time talking to these two, then maybe she'd be saved.

"I meant what I said earlier," Number One informed her. "As soon as I set eyes on those twins coming through that door there, I'll shoot."

Her shoulders sank, as well as her spirits, the fire she'd had in her earlier when she'd contacted the twins gone now, vanished along with any chance she had of receiving help from them. Unless they swept in now with guns themselves, she was on her own against these two.

"Was it your boss who phoned me earlier and came to collect the things in the boxes?" she asked.

"We don't have a boss," Number One said. "But he does pay us for what we do."

"So he chose you for this job, and he chose my café."

"Yeah, and now he's decided, because of your little stunt in involving the twins, that you're surplus to requirements."

She darted her gaze to the door that led to the kitchen, then at her phone on the nearby counter.

"I wouldn't bother," Number Two said from where he sat on a table, swinging his legs as if he didn't care that just his presence alone was so menacing. "My brother will gun you down before you reach either the phone or that door."

My brother. Were these two the twins using fake voices?

No, they couldn't be. When her phone had gone off, neither of them had been using theirs. She supposed that her wishing they were the leaders of the Estate meant she'd have some kind of way to get out of this, because despite the Wilkes twins being abrupt with her whenever they'd spoken, they'd still been nice. It was obvious they had a good side to them, yet *these* men…

"Are you cowards?" she asked in a sudden burst of reckless bravery, something she'd likely regret.

"*What* did you fucking say?" Number One lifted the gun to settle the stock beneath his armpit and aim the muzzle at her.

"Are *you* deaf?" God, where was this courage coming from? Or lunacy. Maybe because she was sick of people like them. Like that bloody Tommy Coda. Blurting stuff out wasn't the smartest thing she'd ever done in her life, but if they planned to kill her, what did it matter *what* she said? They'd made it clear she wouldn't get away from them, so she may as well go down in a blaze of standing-up-for-herself glory. Maybe she'd get lucky and he'd shoot her here, now, so it could all be over quicker.

No, don't give up. Not yet.

"You're one cheeky fucking cow." Number Two got off the table and came over to her, gripping her shoulder and digging his fingertips in. "Get your arse upstairs to pack that bag before I clout you one."

With his hand still on her, his touch vile, she walked into the kitchen and towards the hallway at the back and a door marked PRIVATE. Her legs didn't want to work, and she had to force them to move. He had to let her go when she went up the stairs, but he was right behind her, so close his body heat warmed her. At the top, she had the urge to jump out of one of the windows in her flat, and she would have done if they opened wide enough. As it was, they were the type that only expanded a couple of inches to let in some fresh air, a safety feature she wished didn't exist.

In her bedroom—and she hated him being in there with her, looking at her private space, breathing in it, infecting it—she loaded a small suitcase with wheels that she knew damn well she wouldn't use the contents of. Even if she got out of this alive, she'd ditch the case and everything in it. She wouldn't be able to bear the memories that would come whenever she saw what she'd packed.

She moved past him to go into the bathroom and collect a toothbrush—a new one out of a set-of-three packet she'd bought the other day in Superdrug, when life was so much simpler, despite her helping masked men break the law. Taking a new one was the only way she could alert anyone to the fact that she *hadn't* decided to leave of her own accord. If her original toothbrush was still in the cup on the sink, then maybe it would give someone pause. But that wouldn't be until weeks down the line after she hadn't responded to messages or opened the back door for deliveries, and someone actually bothered to go to the police to report her missing. She'd be long dead by then, but at least someone would be looking for her and perhaps find her body wherever these bastards were going to dump it.

Her legs went to jelly again at that thought. At no point had she ever imagined her life would come to this. Even during the scary time of selling up in France and coming to London, she'd believed everything would be okay. Unless you chose to live in the world of villains, there was no way you'd expect this shit to happen. It happened to other people, bad people, but then that wasn't true, was it? Her involvement in this mess didn't mean it made her a bad person. She was still good, she'd just been forced into complying.

She left the bathroom, closing the door behind her. He loitered on the landing, and she held up the toothbrush to show him what she had in her hand.

"No toothpaste?" he asked on a chuckle.

His nonchalance annoyed her, and she wanted to strike out at him, stab the handle of the toothbrush in his eye, and she could do that, but she had no doubt that he'd recover quickly enough to chase her down the stairs, and then his brother was down there anyway, and he'd catch her. Maybe knock her about a bit to teach her to behave.

"I don't see the point, do you?" she said. "It's not like I'll be brushing my teeth, is it? All this is just a charade in the game you're playing. We both know I'll be dead soon."

He eyed her, head cocked. "You know, I think I might have liked you in other circumstances. You've shown you've got some balls on you. All right, it means you're in this particular situation, because if you'd *juuuust* kept your mouth shut, we wouldn't be here now, but at least you're not one of those insipid bitches who cries about spilt milk. Is that something you've always done, got on with things? I mean, I could tell when my brother told you to pack a bag that it shocked the shit out of you, but you soon got your mettle back, didn't you."

Yes, she had, and she worried that her outburst would come back to bite her on the arse later. She should have stayed meek and mild. "What do you care about what I'm like?"

He shrugged. "Well, you're French, so it kind of makes you a bit more intriguing."

"I don't know why. We all bleed the same no matter where we were born. We all have hopes and dreams."

He nodded. "Hmm. What was your biggest dream?"

She didn't want to tell him, although he *did* look genuinely interested. Maybe there were possibilities with this one. Engaging him in conversation might endear her to him.

"I wanted to have several cafés up and down the country. I wanted your queen, and now your king to eat my pastries." She blushed at how silly that sounded now, but she'd thought about it often, how some man or other in a black suit would turn up in a car and park out the front, dashing into the café to collect a cake box full of her creations for Charles and his wife. Maybe that wouldn't happen in reality. She wouldn't be trusted not to put something dangerous in the biscuits or whatever, but the fantasy had been something to while away the time, and it never hurt to have aspirations.

Number Two took a deep breath. "Do you want to know what mine is?"

She nodded. If they could just find some common ground…

A wide grin appeared in the mask's mouth hole. "To fuck you before I snuff your life out."

The certainty of how foolish she'd been to think he was trying to befriend her crashed down on her so hard she lost her breath. Her naïvety astounded her, and hot tears burned.

He smirked. "I expect you're going to fight when it comes down to the wire, aren't you?"

Anger grabbed her, but she held it back as much as she could. "Again, I don't see the point. If I'm going to end up dead even if I fight, why would I bother?"

"Natural instinct will kick in, you'll see."

The thought of her body trying to save her life when her brain knew it was inevitable she was going to die brought on a wave of sadness and defeat. She leaned against the airing cupboard door, a prominent scene playing out in her head, where she lay on a bed and Number Two loomed over her, his gloved hands around her throat, her clawing at his wrists, trying to get him to let her go.

This wasn't how she thought she'd go out—did *anyone* ever imagine they'd be murdered, for God's sake? Of course not. She'd hoped she'd be over ninety, sitting on a comfortable patio chair with the sun on her face and the birds tweeting when it came time for her to pass over into the next life—and she was glad she believed in the next life now, because it meant that whatever these two did to her, she'd still have a new world waiting on the other side. Not that she'd know about it. She wouldn't be Leanora, she'd be born into someone else's body with no recollection of having been here before, but she'd comfort herself in the knowledge that she *would* exist, somewhere, somehow, so when she took her final breath it wouldn't be so frightening. It wouldn't be the absolute end.

"Hurry up and get your case," he said gruffly as if playtime was over. "We need to get going."

She went back into her room and spied scissors on her vanity table, the blades around five inches long. "I'd better take my makeup bag so it looks authentic. My staff know damn well I won't go anywhere without my face on." She swiped up the bag as well as the scissors and, as she made a show of placing the bag into her suitcase, she slid the scissors beneath the elasticated wristband of her fleece top, the metal chilly against her skin. She didn't glance across to see whether he'd noticed, fearing that would make it obvious she'd done something wrong—wrong in his eyes but completely right in hers.

Now, she had some form of control, a way to save her life.

She zipped up her case and carried it towards him. He jerked his head at her, indicating that she leave the room and go downstairs first. Sensible, because if she had her way and she was behind him, she'd smack her case on the back of his head, then rush down the stairs after him and stab him in the neck while he lay on the floor, stunned. She'd have his brother to contend with afterwards, the shotgun undoubtedly jabbed in her direction, but who was to say there was even any ammunition in it?

She didn't want to take that chance so behaved herself.

At the bottom of the stairs, she stepped out into the little hallway and glanced across at her office, going over there to wait in the doorway. Number Two whistled, and his brother came out of the café and made his way through the kitchen towards them.

He held her phone up, the screen dark. "I've already messaged your workers."

Leanora could imagine what their responses were, if they'd even replied yet. Shocked at her leaving on short notice, the pair of them worrying where they'd find work next. Sally needed the money to help her single-parent mother feed her other kids, so it was going to hit them hard, especially because they relied on the leftover food

Leanora allowed Sally to take home if it couldn't be kept for the following day.

Tears stung her eyes at how that family would now suffer.

"Aww, are you getting emotional?" Number One said. "I would be, too, if I were you. The twins replied. They're arriving here tomorrow at ten. Shame you won't be around to tell them what's what. Mind you, they sounded arsey that you hadn't responded to the first message, or maybe that was my perception."

At least if she couldn't get away from these two by harming them with the scissors, she could go to her grave knowing she'd tried her hardest to get help, to make things right. She'd so wanted to admit her part in storing those boxes and answering the door when the drug customers arrived in the dark, despite knowing the twins would have punished her for it. But her conscience would have been clear. Now she was going to die with the weight of guilt still on her shoulders.

Unless I kill them with the scissors.

And if the twins still come here tomorrow, they might wonder where I am, and anyway, Martin will report back that the café is closed, so it'll look even more worrying. Or did Number One reply to them and say I wouldn't be here?

"What did you say to them?" she asked.

"Nothing. Wait there a second."

"Like I'm going anywhere," Leanora muttered.

"You are," Number Two said, "just not anywhere you want to go." He laughed and moved to the back door, opening it to poke his head out into the yard.

She quickly stuck a finger and thumb under her wristband but had to stop the scissor retrieval when Number One reappeared. Her heart pounded far too hard, and it felt as though the pulse in her neck bulged enough to visibly fluctuate her skin. She stared at what he held, a small white box with the lid open. He'd collected all of the slices of cake that were in the fridge behind the counter.

Better that he had them than they went mouldy eventually.

I hope he chokes.

Number Two brought his head back inside and looked at his brother. "I'll go out the back and check the coast's clear."

He walked outside, and Leanora thought about kicking the door shut while Number One had a hand full of cake and a gun in the other. She could stab him, snatch the gun off him and aim it towards the door for when Number Two came back in.

Had she wasted too much time thinking about it?

Should she go for it now or wait until she was in their vehicle?

The door opened, and Number Two flashed a hand out and grabbed her wrist. He picked up her suitcase and chivvied her out into the yard, then through the open gateway and towards a dark-coloured SUV with blacked-out windows. He pushed her into the back, put her suitcase on the seat next to her, and she closed her eyes to stop herself from seeing how close he was to her. There was movement and a strange clinking noise, so she opened them again to see he'd whipped out a pair of handcuffs. He snapped them around her wrists, and she thanked her lucky stars he hadn't forced her arms behind her back to do it. This way, with her hands in front, she could still get the scissors out. She could still use them.

He leaned over to put her seat belt on, and she had visions of holding the scissors in a double-handed grip and plunging the blades into his cheek. She saw the blood spurting and imagined how hot it would be on her skin where it splashed onto her face. It alarmed her how much that vision pleased her. That scenario wasn't going to work, though, because she'd get her head blown off inside seconds by Number One who stood watching.

Was he wondering what was going through her head?

Did he sense she was planning their murders?

She'd bide her time. Waiting would be to her advantage.

Unfortunately, Number Two got in beside her, dashing her idea of stabbing them both from behind while the car was in motion. He put his own seat belt on while Number One sat in the front, placing the shotgun in the passenger footwell and then revving the engine. She supposed, what with the dark windows, that the pair of them driving around with balaclavas on wouldn't even be noticed. No one would take their phone out and ring the police to say something suspicious was going on, therefore, no one would be saving Leanora anytime soon.

Except herself.

She'd relied on herself for so long now that it was second nature to continue to do so; nothing new there. No, she didn't have the dream love life that Tommy Coda had promised her, but she did have faith that she could survive this now she had a weapon literally up her sleeve.

Where there's hope there's light.

Chapter Seven

LEANORA ARCHAMBEAU: *So you're familiar with the property in question, yes?*

TOMMYCODA: *Yes, I've been doing my shopping along there all my life. It used to be a café before the owner closed it then put it up for sale, so it'll already have everything there for you. I can be your middleman if you like, talking to the owner on your behalf and having a look round the property?*

LEANORA ARCHAMBEAU: *That would be very nice of you, but I couldn't impose.*

TOMMYCODA: *It wouldn't be imposing because I offered. I could at least do the initial visit until you manage to get over here to have a look for yourself. You'll need to be fast because a place like that will be snapped up.*

LEANORA ARCHAMBEAU: *But I don't know you. It seems a bit odd that everything is moving so quickly regarding you.*

TOMMYCODA: *You have to move quickly in this game. [SHRUG EMOJI] If you want to lose out on the place, then that's your problem. I can see how this would seem strange. Someone like me, saying they'll do a lot of the legwork, but there's no catch. I'm not a weirdo, I just want to help. Have a think about it and get back to me. If it helps you can look me up. I own Coda's Cars in South London. There's a picture of me on the website and it matches the one in my profile here. I'll wait.*

LEANORA ARCHAMBEAU: *Oh, okay, I can see it. Wow, you sell high-end cars then?*

TOMMYCODA: *I do indeed. I came on this forum to find a property myself as I'm wanting to expand. I saw your post and thought I'd help, that's all. I know how daunting it can be to find the right place.*

LEANORA ARCHAMBEAU: *I'll email the owner of the café now and let them know I'm interested. If the place is still available, then maybe you can pop round there and have a look at it for me. Take a video?*

TOMMYCODA: *Not a problem. I'll give you my phone number if you fancy chatting in person, as it were.*

LEANORA ARCHAMBEAU: *Here is fine for now.*

TOMMYCODA: *Can't say I blame you for being wary. If I found out some bloke was talking to my mum on the internet, I'd be well suspicious. I expect your dad would be the same with you, wouldn't he?*

LEANORA ARCHAMBEAU: *If he were alive, then yes.*

TOMMYCODA: *Shit, sorry for putting my foot in it.*

LEANORA ARCHAMBEAU: *You didn't. You weren't to know. In case you go and put your foot in it again, my mother is also dead. I was thirteen at the time of the accident. They bought a house to renovate. It was old, falling down basically. They were standing in the kitchen when the ceiling fell on top of them along with all the old furniture the previous owners had stored in that room. My aunt brought me up after that.*

TOMMYCODA: *Bloody hell, that's awful. Are you close to your aunt?*

LEANORA ARCHAMBEAU: *I was until she died, too. It's just me now.*

TOMMYCODA: *I'm really, really sorry.*

LEANORA ARCHAMBEAU: *Life happens. I've just heard back from the café owner. She's willing for you to go round there this afternoon. Is that going to be too soon for you?*

TOMMYCODA: *Absolutely not. What time?*

LEANORA ARCHAMBEAU: *Two.*

TOMMYCODA: *That's brilliant. I'll drive over there now. It takes a while to get from South to East London when the traffic's chocka. I'll send a video when it's done.*

Leanora Archambeau: *Thank you so much for this.*

      Tommy Coda: *You're welcome.*

Chapter Eight

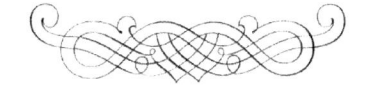

Tommy waited for the Unidenticals. The lock-up was bloody cold with the absence of a radiator. He'd already cursed them in his head a million times for not having a heat source, then had talked himself off the ledge by being practical about it—why *would* they have heat when they were barely there?

He paced up and down past his cocaine, then some other cardboard boxes. One of the top ones had its flaps open, and he stopped to peer inside. Cheap black trainers tied together by the laces. Noel and Joel probably sold shit like this from the back of a lorry, in between doing all of their other jobs. Jacks of all trades, those two.

Tommy slapped his hands together and stamped his feet to try and get some warmth into them, then resumed pacing. Time had seemed to stretch since they'd left, slowing right down. What was keeping them so long? Had Leanora been playing them up, stalling? He wouldn't put it past her, she was a clever bitch, but it annoyed him that even now, in the circumstances she'd found herself in, with the Unidenticals showing up to collect her, she *still* thought she could call the shots.

When she got here, he'd show her she couldn't.

Had the other twins got there first and spirited her away? Had Noel and Joel decided not to tell him the café had been empty? Maybe they were scared of him, deep down. After all, he knew they gadded about pretending to be the Wilkes brothers, and he could get them in the shit for it at any time. Then again, *they* could get *him* in the shit, so perhaps he ought to keep his mind away from thoughts of dobbing them in.

They were better off being friends than enemies.

The rumble of an engine drew him to one side of the wide roller shutter where he stood at a door, took the clown mask out of his pocket, and drew it down over his head and face. He peeked out into the forecourt, blinking at the bright headlights pointing his way. He couldn't make out whether the Unidenticals had parked there or someone else had, so he stepped outside, safe in his disguise, and let the darkness swallow him up when the headlights went off. He stared down at the number plate, not recognising it; the vehicle wasn't their usual one but a black SUV.

He looked up, directly through the tinted windscreen, which was too dark to be legal. The ghostlike shape of Noel nodded to him. A frisson of relief went through Tommy, and he rotated his shoulders to flush out the tension in them, walking around the side of the SUV to the back door, which he opened to find himself confronted with Joel instead of Leanora. Annoyed that the move made him look a complete dickhead, like he didn't know what he was doing, he stalked round to the other side, opened that door, and yanked her out. He let her fall onto the asphalt and glared down at her as she peered up at him.

He wanted her to be bricking it, he'd get a kick out of that, but it seemed fear had either come and gone or she hadn't even felt it yet. Light coming through the lock-up doorway glowed over her. Hatred filled her eyes, and it shouldn't bother him, but it did. He'd spied on her from across the street while she'd worked in the café, just so the last time he'd seen her wouldn't be when she'd walked out on him. Then he had to remind himself she was seeing a man in a clown mask now, and he felt better that her anger wasn't directed at him personally, just at who she thought he was.

He was going to have to change his voice while speaking to her and hoped the Unidenticals didn't give the game away by asking him what he was doing. Surely they'd gather he wanted to keep his identity a secret. But did that really matter? Did her knowing who'd organised all of this, who'd used her, helped her come to London with the promise of love, make a difference when she was going to be killed anyway?

He was going to do it—paying Noel and Joel their exorbitant kill fee wasn't the kind of money he wanted to part with. All he needed was to pay them to collect her, drop her off here, then wait outside while he committed murder so they could warn him if someone else came along. Afterwards, he'd pop her in the back of his van and dump her in Daffodil Woods, and the Unidenticals could clean up any blood that might spill.

But first, he wanted a few words with her.

He bent down and grabbed her by the top of her arm, pulling her to her feet and marching her towards the lock-up. She struggled to get away, so he dug his fingertips into her soft flesh until she cried out. He manhandled her inside, shut the door, and smiled at the idea of the Unidenticals settling down for either a chat or a nap while he did the business.

He threw her to the floor, and she landed on her arse, hanging her head, her breathing laboured. It reminded him of the times he'd fucked her.

"You should have behaved yourself," he said in a gravelly voice, exaggerating his London accent. "You should have continued to do as you were told, then none of this would be happening. But you've probably realised that by now, haven't you? I expect you're regretting going against me, what with hindsight and everything."

He paced around her, loving how it felt to be above her, in control. An eagle circling a mouse. Prey, that's what she was. She glanced up, her hair falling away from her face to show him her expression—she still hated him, more than she had out there on the tarmac. He had the urge to kick her teeth in. Watch her choke on them, gasping for breath. He wanted to wreck her beautiful face with bruises and split lips.

He sniffed at her in disdain. "My mum used to tell me that in order to have no regrets I needed to stop and think for ten seconds before making a big decision. It doesn't always work, sometimes I leap before I look, but for the most part, I plan everything out. If I have a knee-jerk reaction and do or say something I shouldn't, then I rectify it as soon as possible, which is something you should have done. You should have messaged the twins and said you didn't need to chat with them anymore, then phoned me back to say you'd realised the error of your ways and I didn't need to come round to collect those boxes. But you didn't. You didn't think for ten seconds. Silly cow."

She remained where she was, her hair falling forward to hide her face again, not that he wanted to see it at the moment. He wasn't sure whether he still wanted to punch the fuck out of it or kiss her. Force her to have sex with him one last time. Show her exactly who was in control.

I'm no rapist, and anyway, I don't have any condoms on me.

"Where are the other two?" she asked.

Her accent stirred his dick. "Out in their car. Why?"

"One of them said he was going to have sex with me and then kill me."

What was she playing at? Lying, seeing what the pecking order was? Was she waiting for Tommy to get angry, storm out to the Unidenticals to tell them off, leaving her in the perfect position to get away? Was she gauging the situation, like any normal person would, checking out her options?

Or had one of them really said that?

"That was just a scare tactic to get you to go with them," he said. "It's me who has the choice to do that, not them."

Did a shudder just go through her?

He smiled at her being revolted at the thought of a clown-masked man violating her and then ending her life. Now he wished he could see her face and the fear on it. Or was she wearing her own mask by now, hiding any expression that would give him an inkling as to what she was feeling?

He stepped over to her, gripped the back of her fleece top, and put her on her feet. He turned her so she faced him, roughly pushing the hair out of her eyes, and saw nothing but defiance looking back at him. She was going to go down fighting. Could he be bothered with that? He didn't particularly relish torture or beating the shit out of people, he preferred to chat and get things smoothed over quickly. Despite his hatred of her for having the guts to leave him, he wasn't irate enough with her anymore to draw this out.

She breathed heavily, her shoulders going up and down, the sheen of sweat on her face the only indication that anger boiled her from the inside out. It was too cold in here for her to be warm enough to overheat from the air. He smirked at what must be going through her mind. How she was likely thinking of ways to get out of here. Hitting him then running for the door, even knowing the men who'd brought her here waited outside. It would be natural for her to want to live, and the courage to do that would come from somewhere.

He took a deep breath to say what he had to say. "You really are—"

Her handcuffed arms flashed up. Something glinted in her hand as she arced it towards him, and a sharp sting pierced his mask and then his cheekbone. She'd taken him by surprise by acting so quickly, and his brain hadn't yet caught up with the action. Then it did, and anger spiked. He shoved her chest. She staggered backwards, crying out, perhaps in frustration. A drip of what he assumed was blood coursed down his cheek, and he lunged forward, casting a glance at what she held.

A pair of scissors.

Where the fuck had she got *those* from? The Unidenticals must have taken their eye off her in order for her to have hidden them. What the hell was he paying them for when they couldn't do their job properly?

Her eyes glinted with malice. God knows what his were revealing—maybe the same? They circled one another, him orchestrating that manoeuvre on purpose, and at the point her back faced the boxes of trainers, he pushed her again. She stumbled in reverse and landed on her arse, his hope of her dropping the scissors dashed when he caught sight of them still clutched in her fingers. He darted to the left and stuffed his hand into the top box, grabbing a trainer and hauling it and its tied-up companion out. Her exhalations barged between her lips noisily, and as she quickly rose to standing, he darted behind her, his mind a few steps ahead:

She was well able to jerk her hand backwards to stab him.

She could spin any second now and ram those blades into his gut.

But he didn't give her the chance. With a trainer in each hand, he yanked them away from each other so the knotted-together laces lengthened, then looped them over her head to press the taut strip against her neck. He pulled the trainer soles towards one another behind her head, and the sound of the scissors clanking on the floor gave him a rush of satisfaction. She sagged, likely in an attempt to get her throat away from the noose, but he lowered with her, drawing the trainer soles completely together. It created the perfect tightness on her throat. He held on for what felt like an age, until the life ebbed out of her, then she flopped and he let her fall to the floor. She lay on her back, a trainer either side of her head, the knotted laces draped across it over a livid red line.

He stared at her chest to check for breathing.

It didn't move.

He backed off, leaning against the roller shutter to get his composure back. He didn't bother looking at her to savour what he'd done—so long as she was dead and no longer a threat, that was all that mattered, and if he were truly honest, he didn't feel good about himself.

Being a killer didn't make him feel as powerful as he'd thought.

It took him a moment to process his actions. The strangulation. The way she'd all but collapsed. He'd read strangulation took at least four minutes to make someone brain dead but seconds to render them unconscious. Was that all she was, asleep? Or had she had a heart attack?

He stared at her chest again.

Nothing.

Back on an even keel, he opened the door to check outside. No other vehicles had arrived, and the Unidenticals were still in their SUV. He picked her up, double-checking the floor to make sure the scissors were still there and she hadn't picked them up when he wasn't looking, then carried her out to his van. He dumped her in the back on top of an old sleeping bag, locking the doors, and went to pay Noel and Joel.

Noel opened the driver's-side window. "That was fast. Did you get excited and shoot your load too quickly?"

Tommy shook his head, frowning at them, but remembered they wouldn't be able to see his face because of the mask. "I didn't go anywhere near her like that. I got the job done, end of." He took an envelope out of his coat pocket and handed it over. "This is for the floor space rental plus the money for going to collect that bitch—oh, and some of my blood might be in there on a pair of scissors she must have brought with her from the café—as in neither of you noticed she had them on her. She nicked my cheek. I'll let my drug man know that the delivery needs to come here in future until I find somewhere else. Shall I get him to contact you directly so you can be here when it arrives?"

Noel nodded. "Give him our burner number. Did you let tonight's customers know they had to come this way?"

"Yeah. I said the meeting place is round the corner by that big tree."

"What time?"

"Midnight."

"Right. Where's she going to end up?"

"Daffodil."

Noel pressed the button for the window to go up. Tommy got in his van and peered between the front seats to check on Leanora. She lay exactly where he'd left her—of course she fucking did, she was dead—and as he backed out of the forecourt, he congratulated himself on a job well done, even though revenge didn't taste sweet.

He swallowed down the bitterness and headed for the woods.

Chapter Nine

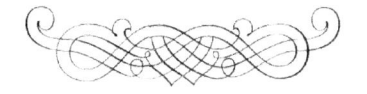

In the murky light of the March morning, George stood outside the French Café, annoyed Leanora hadn't responded to any of his messages, nor had she opened the door to his many polite-at-first knocks—or subsequent arsey thumps to the glass. As it was just after ten o'clock now, she should have opened the café a good while ago, but when he and Greg had arrived, a line of customers had been waiting. George had told them to bugger off, receiving some filthy looks, but as he didn't want to create any fuss or draw any more attention to himself, he hadn't reprimanded anyone. Greg was currently round the back trying to get inside.

George's hopes rose when the blind on the door flapped slightly, then the sound of a safety chain being drawn across filtered out. The lock pick had obviously done its job at the rear. The door opened, Greg standing in the slim gap, his expression grim. George took it that his brother wasn't too happy about something he'd discovered. Had Leanora been found harmed? Was it time for George to feel guilty that he hadn't pushed her for more information last night, phoning her when she hadn't WhatsApped him back? Should they have popped by here before they'd gone to the Taj, just to make sure she was okay?

He shut the door behind him and raised his eyebrows.

"She's not here," Greg said. "I've even checked upstairs."

"Any signs of a struggle?"

"No."

"Didn't she tell us she had no family?"

"Yep. She also said the flat upstairs was vacant because she lived at a boyfriend's house, but it's clear she's been living upstairs—or someone has."

"What if she got a tenant in and they turned funny on her? That could be why she said she needed to talk to us."

Greg shrugged.

George followed him through the café and into a kitchen, then out into a short hallway. He remembered having their first chat with her in the office, and to be honest, he hadn't really taken much notice of his surroundings. At the time, all he'd been bothered about was giving her their spiel about what protection money meant for her, he'd shit her up a bit to make his point, and then they'd left her to it. The only other time they'd come here was a month after she'd arrived where George had reinforced their message and, as it was obvious she'd clearly accepted it, he felt no more visits where necessary unless Martin told them otherwise.

Now, he wished he'd popped in on her more. Learned more about her. At least got the name of the boyfriend who could be contacted in emergencies, especially because she'd mentioned having no family. Once again, he'd dropped the ball, perhaps in his cockiness that he believed he always had things under control or maybe because he'd been too impatient to get out of here and move on to the next job. Either way, he needed to really think before he made decisions in the future, something Greg had requested he do to save them hassle farther down the line.

But Greg's just as culpable. He didn't ask for the name of an emergency contact either.

Feeling better that his brother shared the blame and that if his twin dared to bring up the lapse in judgement he had something to fling back in his face, George took the stairs and had a nose around the flat. He started with the bathroom, and a toothbrush in a cup indicated she hadn't planned to go anywhere. In her bedroom, the quilt was ruffled in one place, and a rectangular imprint had been left behind beside it, as if she'd placed a box on it. He checked inside the wardrobe for a suitcase and found a large one, but it didn't match the size of the shape on the bed.

He rooted around in the living room and the kitchen; nothing untoward appeared to have happened, so why did he have an uneasy feeling in his gut? He'd been annoyed with her last night when she hadn't responded to his messages, when all along something might have been happening to her. Of course, she might well have just taken off for the day, shutting the café to give herself some 'me time', and in order to do that, she'd have had to contact her employees to tell them not to come in.

Doesn't she trust them to run the place for a day without her?

Back downstairs, he found Greg in her office rifling through papers in a drawer.

"When we came here before," George asked, "did you clock who worked here with her?"

"Yeah, the girl is Sandra Deptford's kid, her eldest, she does the washing up and waitressing. The lad who makes the sandwiches is Harley Jones, Adam Jones' kid, the bloke who owns the scrapyard we used from time to time back in the day."

"Then we'll need to get hold of them."

"We'll leave out the back way so I can use the pick to lock up."

George secured the front door then tailed him out into the yard. While Greg got on with click-clacking the lock into place, George mooched around to find any evidence of foul play. No spots of blood had dripped on the patio slabs, and the yard was empty so nothing had been pushed over, maybe in Leanora's attempt to alert someone that something bad had happened.

But this all might be innocent. Calm down.

In their BMW, Greg gunned the engine. "We'll start with the scrapyard, it'll save us from asking too many questions of our street snitches. I don't want people getting wind that the café is empty. You know what some people are like, they'll think nothing of robbing the place."

They reached the scrapyard inside five minutes, and George got out, heading for a Portakabin. He tapped on the door and then entered, nodding to Adam who sat up a little straighter, his eyebrows raised.

"What can I do for you?" Adam asked, clearly wary.

"Where's your son?"

Adam's expression darkened, a reaction to his fatherly instincts coming to the fore. Regardless of it being George standing in front of him, it was obvious he'd go to bat for his kid despite any risks.

"He'll be at work, like usual."

"Where?"

"The French Café first thing, then he moves on to another sandwich shop after, Between the Slices."

"The French Café's closed, and we're concerned about the owner."

Adam relaxed, his features smoothing out now he'd realised the issue wasn't with Harley. "Oh, that doesn't sound good. Anything I can do to help?"

"You can get your boy on the blower and tell him I want a chat."

Adam took a phone out of his pocket and prodded at the screen. He held the mobile to his ear. "All right, boy? Listen, I've got one of The Brothers here. No, no, I haven't done anything wrong, like I even would, so don't you go worrying. George wants to talk to you about one of your bosses. Her from the French Café. Did she? Oh, then you'd better tell him that."

He handed the phone over, and George took it.

"What have you got for me?" he asked.

"I got a message from her last night, saying she was going to France. I wrote back and asked her if everything was okay and when she'd be back, but she didn't answer me. It's all right because I've got another place I make sandwiches for, but not knowing how long she's going to be gone for… I might have to find more work somewhere else."

"What time did she message you?"

Harley let him know, and George had a little think. That would have been when they were still eating in the Taj—they'd remained there for a good while. So what had been going on between George responding to her message after they'd been to Moon's and her sending one to Harley?

"Do you happen to know the phone number or address of the girl who works with you?" Again, it would save them asking around because although George knew of the family, he wasn't one hundred percent sure where they lived.

"Sally? Yeah, she's at number three Alding Close."

Ah, that shithole area where the fuckers are a bit lawless. "Cheers, and keep this conversation under your hat. If the café's being left empty, we don't want anyone knowing she's not there."

George handed the phone back to Adam, nodded his thanks, then left the Portakabin. Greg stood talking to some bloke in dirty overalls about the merits of alloy wheels. George gave his twin a pointed look, and Greg quickly left the man to his job.

They both got in the car.

"Alding Close," George said. "I spoke to Harley. Leanora told him she was going to France. If she was doing that, why didn't she take her toothbrush and the big suitcase in her bedroom—or let us know she wouldn't be there when we popped by at ten or when Martin collects the money? She knows the fucking rules."

"Hmm, but maybe that's why she needed to speak to us—to tell us she's off to France."

"But she didn't respond to me, and that's a worry. I'll get hold of Colin to see if he can make discreet enquiries at the ferry terminals and airports." He sent that message off then stared through the windscreen. "Something's off, and I'm angry with myself for not feeling this way last night."

"She didn't exactly sound upset in her message. There was no clue that she needed help, just that she wanted to talk—which could have been about any number of things. If something's happened, that's not on you. We're not psychic, we can't tell from what she said that something was going on, *if* it even is. The logical situation is she could have wanted to talk to us about going back to France, you didn't reply, she had to get going to catch a flight or whatever, and she'll get hold of us when she's got a moment."

This was why it was good to talk out his feelings. George felt better now his brother had put things into perspective, yet that niggle still remained inside him, but that could be because the riddle hadn't been solved, and unsolved riddles had always pissed him off ever since they'd been kids.

"I still want to get to the bottom of this," he said, "so I'll give her a ring now."

She didn't answer.

"She could be asleep," Greg suggested. "All that travelling."

"True, and fuck it, I forgot to ask Harley if he knows who the boyfriend is."

"Then we'll ask Sally."

Greg entered the close, and at George's indication towards number three, he parked outside it. A few front gardens—a few too many—had junk in them, although it might have been placed outside for the council to collect. At least it had better be. The street looked a right state with those fridges and whatnot there. No wonder it had got itself a bad name.

They left the car and walked up the garden path, George knocking on the door a bit too loudly—his aggravation was showing. The shadow of someone coming to answer appeared through the mottled glass. George judged it to be the shape of a small, slim person. The door opened, and a young blonde girl of maybe nineteen, twenty stood there, her eyes widening dramatically when she saw who stood on the path.

"Has something happened to Leanora?" she asked.

"Why would you ask that?"

"I shouldn't really tell you. I was told to keep my mouth shut."

"Who by?"

"Two blokes in balaclavas. They came to the café yesterday, told me to go home and pretend I never saw them."

"What did they want?"

"To talk to Leanora. One of them had a shotgun."

"And you didn't think to get hold of us?"

"Like I said, I was told not to. I was *scared*, okay?"

"Right."

"And that France thing is a bit weird and I'm not buying it. She texted me to say that's where she was going. I had a change of heart and nearly rang the police this morning but then thought I was better off talking to you. I was just about to get my shoes and coat on and go to The Angel to let Lisa know I needed a chat. I heard that's what you have to do, speak to her an' that."

Hmm, was she only making out she was going to tell them this little story because of how angry George must look? Was she saving face?

She glanced up and down the street. "You'd best come in, the neighbours are well nosy."

She took them into a kitchen at the back and, while they sat at a table in a cramped corner surrounded by piles of washing in baskets, she leaned against the edge of the worktop and hugged herself.

"Did you want a cuppa or anything?"

"Unless you have a Tassimo machine, then no ta," George said.

"Nah, we haven't got anything like that. So what's going on? And I don't want to be rude or nothing, but can we be quick because I need to find another job. Mum struggles, see, because my dad died and left her with three kids. Things are a bit tight."

George frowned. "Why didn't you come to us? We help pay for funerals and have a fund for those in need. Alternatively, we could have used your mum as a pair of ears and eyes and she'd get paid for it. She still could. Where is she now?"

"At work down the covered market. She sweeps up and stuff like that, then she picks my brother and sister up from school, makes the dinner, and then when I get home from the café she goes out to a cleaning job every evening except Sundays."

"Then we'll be back to speak to her around five, assuming she'll be home then."

Alding Close was a street where lots of petty thieves and scutty fuckers lived, so the mother would be an excellent person to employ to watch the goings-on and report back. She'd have to give up work so she was on hand to spy all day, making out she'd gone on benefits, but whatever George and Greg paid her would be more than she'd get for slogging her guts out for someone else.

Sally nodded. "I can message her now if you like."

"Go on then. Tell her there's a grand a week on offer, and if she wants to get her arse back here now to talk about it, then she can, but she'll have to be quick because we need to find out where Leanora is."

Sally prodded a message into her phone, and it bleeped back almost immediately. "She's taking her lunch break early and will be here in a bit."

"Okay. So you said this France thing was weird. What did you mean by that?"

"I know I don't look like the sort of person Leanora would confide in, but she hasn't got any friends here, and I suppose because I work with her all day she let a few things slip. When she lived in France she got chatting to this bloke online. His name's Tommy but I don't know what his surname is. Anyway, he got hold of her on this forum where she asked the group if there were any cafés that would become vacant soon in

England because she wanted to open a place here. He got talking to her and said there was one in London. There was a lot of back and forth, and he convinced her to come over and live with him."

"Were they romantically involved by that point?" Greg asked.

"Yeah, he proper charmed her, didn't he. She lived at his house for a while, then one day she told me she'd left him and moved into the flat upstairs."

"How come?" George narrowed his eyes.

"She reckoned he'd turned into a control freak. Anyway, there were a lot of things that flapped the old red flags, so she broke it off. Now I'm worried something's happened to her. There was this documentary I watched once, right, and this fella, he used his girlfriend's phone to tell everyone she was going backpacking when really he'd put her body in a septic tank."

Fuck me sideways, this kid's got an imagination.

"While my mind hasn't quite gone to septic tanks yet," George said, "I do share your concern. Now then, I need you to keep this to yourself. No gossiping about what might have happened. If there's something bad going on, then we want to keep it on the downlow. We don't want to alert anyone who may be involved that we know about her so-called buggering off."

"You're scaring me. What if those men hurt her?"

George smiled. "Then I'll fucking kill them."

He was saved any more conversation by the slam of the front door and a bustle of movement as a skinny blonde woman in a fake fur coat came into the kitchen. She must have got a cab to have arrived so soon.

She looked from Sally to the twins. "What's going on?"

Sally filled her in, then finished with: "I said it was weird, didn't I? I knew she wouldn't just go back to France like that."

"She might well have done," George said, "maybe to get away from this Tommy bloke and the other men, and we could all be panicking for nothing, so let's calm down and discuss the reason your mum's here." He smiled at Sandra. "How do you feel about spying on your neighbours, love?"

Chapter Ten

Tommy walked around the café and assumed it was exactly what the Frenchwoman needed. It was exactly what **he** *needed, and that was all that mattered, so as he took the video while the owner, Mrs Blanchard, waited out the front (she needed air due to having a hot flush), he gave a running commentary into the speaker to big the place up for Leanora.*

"Nice kitchen area. Saying that, you might be used to a larger space, but it looks okay to me. Mrs Blanchard said she's happy to sell you the ovens and whatnot in with the price, so I reckon you're getting a good bargain to be honest." He walked towards a door at the back and opened it, stepping out into a hallway. *"Let's have a nose in these other rooms, shall we?"*

He did the full tour, including the flat upstairs, and ended up back in the café itself so she could see the size of it and how many tables it contained. He added that he thought she could add more without customers feeling too cramped.

"So what do you think?" He turned the phone around so it filmed his face. He wanted her to trust him. He needed her to take this place on. That storeroom and the location were perfect for what he had in mind. *"Talk to you online later."* He ended the video.

He pulled the blind back on the front door and caught Mrs Blanchard's eye.

She came back inside, flapping a hand in front of her face. "I'm that boiling. God, you ought to count yourself lucky you're not a woman, lad. The shit we have to go through. Even on HRT I'm a sodding sweaty mess."

Tommy beamed at her to hide the revolting imagery she'd just given him—a damp hairline and wet underboob skin. "I'll just upload this video and send it to Leanora. I think this is exactly what she wants, so hopefully she'll get back to you soon. Thanks very much for letting me have a look around, I really appreciate it."

The woman's ruddy cheeks gave away exactly what she was going through. Her hormones were likely all over the place. She nodded and followed him out onto the street. "Oh, that's better, fresher air. I could live in the North Pole I'm that roasting."

He reckoned he was going to have to acknowledge her overheated state in order for her to shut up about it. "My mum's going through what you are. She says liquid talc works wonders. You know, so she doesn't feel so sweaty."

"Thanks for that tip, love, I'll look into it. I bet it's lovely on the inner thighs."

Tommy felt sick.

She sighed, staring at the front of the café. "I'm sad to be selling the place, but my son and his wife have moved to Australia. She's pregnant, and I won't get to see my grandchild much if I stay here, so he suggested I go out there. To be honest, I didn't think they'd want me, but he's been insistent. I've sold the house, just got to get rid of this place now."

"Did you not live upstairs then?"

She locked the door and shook her head. "No, I rented it out to tenants. A lovely couple, and I didn't really want to let them down by selling up, but I've got to think of myself, and living in London on my own wasn't a happy prospect. I'll be letting Leanora know that I'll knock some money off the asking price if she's really that interested—the quicker I sell, the quicker I can bugger off."

"That's very kind of you."

They shook hands and went their separate ways, Tommy smiling to himself. It sounded like this deal was in the bag, so he'd get hold of the Unidenticals and broker a deal of his own. In the car, he sent a message to organise a meet and, given the green light, he drove to their lock-up. He tapped on the door and went inside.

"To what do we owe the pleasure?" Noel asked.

Tommy explained what he wanted. He couldn't be arsed to keep getting up in the middle of the night to sell drugs anymore. He needed to delegate, give up some control. And besides, it was getting too risky.

"So do you think you can do it?" he asked.

Noel's eyebrows met in the middle. "How come you're not selling drugs from the showroom anymore?"

Tommy didn't want to have to explain. He thought that the fact he needed them to do the job for him and that he'd pay them was enough information. Obviously not. "The manager I employ asks a lot of questions about why the alarm has been switched off in the middle of the night and what I was doing on the CCTV with people at the back door. I mean, I could just tell him to mind his own fucking business and that I'm selling cars at night because some customers prefer it, but then he'd think the customers were dodgy, and that I'm dodgy, and he might end up getting hold of the police. So I made out they were mates who'd come to collect some brochures I'd had printed and they were going to distribute them to generate more custom."

Joel scoffed. "Do you seriously think he believed that story?"

"I've just got to hope he does." Tommy sighed. "I've been leaving the running of the showroom to him, letting him oversee the other lad and teaching him the ropes, so he's holed up in the office being a lazy bastard and nosing on the footage instead of doing his actual job."

Noel shook his head. "Maybe he was doing his actual job, as in checking the cameras to make sure no one's been snooping around the forecourt overnight and he just happened to see you at the back door with customers. You ought to be grateful he's so vigilant."

That was a fair point, although at the time when Lionel had told him what he'd discovered on the footage, Tommy had wanted to punch his bastard lights out. That wouldn't have been fair, though. Tommy only had himself to blame for forgetting to switch the cameras off while he was there. The one time he hadn't done it, and Lionel had discovered his secret.

Thank God the footage deleted itself after thirty-six hours, else Lionel would have seen a damn sight more 'pamphlet collecting' if he'd gone back in time.

"Whatever, but as you can imagine, I'm going to need a new place to sell the drugs from," Tommy said. "I've already accidentally on purpose broken the CCTV at the showroom and I'll get it fixed again after the new location has been set up at the café. I don't trust Lionel not to check the times I've turned the alarm off and on, and now check if I switched the cameras off at some point, so selling from the showroom is out. Actually, what I could do is meet the buyers down the road a bit in that little forest round the back."

"Selling from behind trees will make you feel like a run-of-the-mill drug dealer instead of the more upmarket one you reckon you are."

Tommy resisted telling Noel to fuck right off. "Because of Lionel, I haven't got any other option."

"Sack the cunt," Joel said. "Problem solved."

"You do realise it could be ages before this French bint moves over here, don't you?" Noel said. "I mean, this Blanchard woman might want the sale to go through quickly, but the cogs don't turn too fast when it comes to buying property. Are you going to stand in the dark behind a tree in the middle of the night for God knows how long to sell your gear?"

"No, I'm going to break into the café using a lock pick and sell from there." The idea had just hit Tommy out of the blue, and it was a bloody good one, even if he did say so himself. "I talked to Blanchard about the CCTV and any measures she's taken to keep the place secure now that it's empty. She hasn't got an alarm system, which is bloody stupid but to my advantage."

"What if the French woman doesn't buy the café?"

"Then I'll use it for as long as I can then move on."

Noel eyed him. "So you're going to store the drugs in a café where the owner could come in and discover them at any time?"

Tommy cursed himself for thinking exactly that. "Of course not. What do you take me for?"

"So you're going to drive around with bricks of coke in your van prior to handing them over, are you?"

"I haven't had time to figure it all out."

"How about you cease selling drugs until the café's been sold?"

Tommy shook his head. "There are going to be people who won't be too happy about that."

"Then get rid of Lionel," Joel suggested again. "It's simple. If you don't trust him to stop being nosy, then he has to go."

Tommy couldn't fault that logic, but Lionel was a bloody good car salesman, and he didn't fancy letting him go. "Right, just so I'm aware, if I can get the café situation up and running, are you up for meeting the customers there in my place? It means a lot of sales during the night, though."

Noel nodded. "We'll do it for a price, yeah."

Tommy smiled. "That's all I needed to hear."

Chapter Eleven

Leonora woke in the dark. The sense of being *inside* somewhere was so strong, yet she couldn't work out where. Birds twittered. Was she still asleep, dreaming? She became more aware. Something lay on top of her, not heavy but enough for her to know it was there, and she focused her eyes. She appeared to be inside fabric; it was all around her, her head enclosed. Frightened, she went to move an arm but found her wrists were locked together. She reached over and patted either side to try and find a way out, maybe a zip? She couldn't locate one and had to force herself to lie on her back and breathe deeply to get her emotions under control.

The fabric touching her face felt scary.

Her pulse thudded loudly, and she worked hard to slow her careening mind, which wanted to take her on a panic journey—but at least she'd recognised that in time, otherwise she imagined she'd be thrashing around like a wild animal.

She blew out a long breath.

Why am I here?

How did I get here?

What happened to me?

Last night forced its way into her head, and she wished she hadn't asked those questions of herself so she could have remained oblivious. It all flashed in snippets, quick-fire scenes.

The man in the clown mask strangling her with something.

Her pretending to be dead.

Him carrying her and putting her in that van.

A short journey.

Him parking and taking her out into the cold.

Her opening her eyes slightly.

Darkness, the trees, the sliver of moon between two trunks.

Him dropping her on the ground.

Her playing dead again.

Oh my fucking God…

An involuntary whimper had come out of her—she remembered wanting to scream at herself over it—then the rustle of his footsteps on the mulchy ground had come towards her, getting louder and louder.

He'd hit her on the forehead with something, and she'd screamed in pain, then his hand had slapped over her mouth to shut her up—so were they somewhere other people were around? Had he worried she'd be heard and someone would come to investigate? Was she still in the same place now?

He'd wedged his thumb beneath her nostrils, and once again she'd had her air supply cut off, the same as she had in that place Numbers One and Two had taken her to. She'd sagged quicker this time, holding her breath, then she'd had to breathe shallowly and hope the clown wasn't watching her chest to see if it was going up and down.

He'd manhandled her into a sleeping bag, she recalled it so vividly now. Her panic had subsided—unless he was going to throw her in the river or he'd put her in the bag because he couldn't bear to see her face when he killed her, then surely she'd survive this.

The crunch of his footsteps as he'd moved away had been a relief, and she'd dared to hope that he was leaving her, not going off to get another weapon. She'd lain there for such a long time that she must have fallen asleep. Maybe the blow to her head had been a major factor in her being able to drop off. Had he taken her elsewhere after that?

What time was it now? As it was dark inside the bag, she couldn't tell. She tried again to find a zip, finally locating it then tracing the line of it with a finger until she found a gap. She poked her finger through and felt around for the slider, grasping it and pulling it along to create a bigger opening.

Daylight. Beautiful sunshine.

She squinted, made an even larger hole, and sat up, pushing the bag down to her waist. The sleeping bag appeared old, well-used, grubby. She stared around at what Clown Mask must have thought would be her last location prior to her body being found and placed on a post-mortem table. There were lots and lots of trees in an area where she couldn't discern any pathways, so he'd put her out of sight in a tucked-away thicket. She rolled over several times to move along the ground.

A clearing on the other side of a sparse-leafed bush.

Tyre tracks in the mud.

Did he realise he'd left proof of him being here, or at least his vehicle? Or didn't he care? There'd be evidence on his tyres, too, the mud could be matched to this location.

She undid zip all the way round and stood to drape the sleeping bag around her in a cloak-like fashion, finding it awkward with her wrists bound by…by handcuffs, oh God. She stumbled towards the clearing, her eyes sore, as though the bash to her brow had affected them in some way. It could be the light, though. Her head pounded to the beat of the blood rushing through her more quickly than it had when she'd been lying down. She went giddy for a moment and reached out to steady herself on a tree trunk, the bark rough on her palms. In the clearing, she skirted the tyre tracks so they weren't disturbed, then followed the patterns in the ground beyond where he must have driven the van away. Eventually, they led to a tarmac area where cars were parked.

An elderly man got out of one of them and moved to his boot.

Her stomach rolled over. What if this was Clown Man, coming back to collect her body? No, that was stupid, because if he wanted to dispose of her elsewhere, he wouldn't have brought her here in the first place. And as for collecting her in daylight…no one would be so stupid.

He opened the boot, and a large whippet or lurcher jumped out, light-grey fur and a white stripe on its nose. It spotted Leanora and bolted towards her, tongue lolling, its owner calling out in an attempt to get him back. She made eye contact with the man and saw the exact moment he registered that things weren't normal.

"Oh deary me, are you okay?" he asked, coming closer but staying far enough away, perhaps so she wouldn't be spooked.

The dog had no such manners. It jumped up at her, planting its paws on her chest and trying to lick her face. She laughed despite being in such a weird and surreal situation.

"Do you want me to phone the police?" he asked.

She shook her head. "No. The Brothers."

"Oh, um… I don't know how to get hold of them, I'm afraid."

"Ring The Angel," she said and sank to the ground as another wave of giddiness pulled her under.

Chapter Twelve

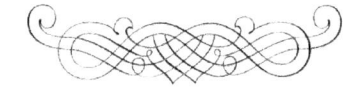

Clifford Rodney didn't know what to do. He ought to ring for an ambulance really—it wasn't every day that a bloodied woman with a French accent fainted in front of him—but she'd mentioned The Brothers, and even though he'd never had a reason to cross their path, nor Ron Cardigan's before them, he knew enough to know that if she didn't want the police involved and she needed the twins, then it was in his best interests to do as he was told.

Still, he dithered. Truth be told, he wanted to get the dog in the car and go home, pretend he hadn't seen this woman or that the hassle that was bound to come with her hadn't disrupted his morning. He tended to keep himself to himself these days, since his wife had died, because he'd found having other people in his life brought irritations he didn't want, need, and nor could he cope with them, not anymore. Not without Ida who'd been his rock, the one who'd dealt with any inconveniences for him. She'd always joked that *he* should be the one to die first because she'd be absolutely fine to continue on without him, she could organise things much better than he ever would, where as he…couldn't. Wasn't any good at this living alone lark.

A surge of annoyance shot upwards through his body—it was so unfair that his weekly walk here had been interrupted by something he couldn't ignore. It was bad enough that when he saw other dog walkers he had to nod in greeting, as if it was the law. He did it in a way that told them he wasn't in the mood to stop and talk. It had been something he'd had to perfect, because at first they'd wanted to chatter away as though he had all the time in the world to listen to *their* problems (just because he was old, so therefore, he couldn't possibly be busy?), but when it came time for *him* to have a turn, talking about Ida being gone, how crushingly lonely it was, they didn't want to know.

It was better that he didn't interact with anyone if he could help it.

But that option wasn't going to solve his current predicament. Much as he did just want to drive away, he couldn't. This looked too serious for that.

His lurcher, Fidel, pranced around the fallen woman, then whimpered and lay beside her, resting his head on hers as though they were best friends. The bloody animal was a sod for being overfriendly, although Clifford couldn't deny it, Fidel had been amazing since Ida's death, a great source of comfort. He didn't know what he would have done without him.

Clifford moved closer, relieved her chest rose and fell and that his first impression of an actual *hole* in her forehead had been incorrect—*my God, I thought she'd been shot.* It was clear someone had hit her with something, or she'd fallen and bumped it, but it was only a shallow gash that had bled. When he'd first set eyes on her and the blood streaks down her face, his chest had tightened like it had when he'd had a heart attack last year.

What he wouldn't give to turn the clock back and not have to deal with this.

He used his phone to look up The Angel's number, then rang it.

"Good morning, The Angel, Lisa speaking."

"Um, you don't know me, but I've just come to Daffodil Woods with my dog, and there's this woman. She's fainted now and—"

"Urm, call an ambulance?"

"Well, I would, but she told me to phone for The Brothers."

"Oh, right, then that's a different story. Daffodil Woods, yes?"

"Yes, at the car park."

"Stay there."

The line went dead.

Fidel looked up at him.

"Help will be here soon," Clifford said, then jumped at the fluttering of the woman's eyelashes. If he were completely honest, he'd rather she stayed asleep because then he wouldn't have to engage with her. He didn't mean that in a nasty way, but his doctor had told him to avoid stress as much as possible. Stress was a killer, and now he'd found some way to live without Ida—an impossibility, he'd once thought—he didn't much want to be dead.

She pushed herself to a sitting position—*oh Lord, handcuffs*—and Fidel clambered onto her lap, all gangly legs and draping tongue. She stroked him and stared into the middle distance, blinking. What had happened to her? What was going through her mind?

"Um, I phoned The Angel," Clifford said, "and the lady told me to stay here."

The woman nodded.

"What's your name?"

She paused as though contemplating whether to tell him. For all she knew, he could be a nasty man out to do her some more damage, so he completely understood her reticence.

"Leanora."

Ah, so she trusted him then? He wasn't sure whether to be happy about that or not. Trusting someone meant you leaned on them more, and he most certainly didn't want her to do *that*.

"How did you hurt your head?" he asked.

"Someone…someone tried to kill me last night."

Oh, dear God. What am I supposed to say to that?

Clifford glanced around, panicking now—what if they were being watched? An awful creepy feeling stole over him, and then he had a terrible thought. What if this was one of those tricks like he'd read about in the paper, when one person acted as though they'd been hurt and then someone else jumped out and robbed whoever had stopped to help? What if they hurt Fidel? Clifford whistled, needing his dog close by, but the animal ignored him, clearly thinking Leanora's need was greater than his master's.

She drew what he could now make out was an open sleeping bag closer around her. Fidel jumped off her lap and then resettled there on top of the material.

"How dreadful for you," Clifford said, telling himself to remain calm, all the while darting his gaze around in case the killer lurked nearby.

"He put me in this sleeping bag and then drove off."

Clifford tried to work out whether this *was* one of those scams. She'd sounded convincing enough, but then these people did, didn't they? There were beggars who looked like beggars but were no such thing. There were those who knocked on the front door selling cloths and such, pretending they were just out of prison and trying to earn a living, when really they were sometimes cowboys casing your home to see when it would be empty. Then there were those symbols gangs had taken to putting on front doors and on the backs of cars to let other members know they were ripe for robbing. The world had turned into a dreadful place. You couldn't trust anyone these days, so why should he trust her?

He cleared his throat. "Goodness, have you been out all night?"

"I must have been, but I was asleep?"

Why had she said it as a question? Didn't she know if she'd slept or not? Was he supposed to believe her? This was all so bloody *odd*. Then again, if she really *had* been hit on the head, then perhaps it had knocked her out.

Not knowing all the facts brought on a worrying flutter in his chest. "Do you know who the man was?"

"He had a clown mask on."

"Oh my word…" This was all a bit much for Clifford, and he fanned his face as a flush of heat suffused his cheeks. "Err, um…why did he want to kill you?" *Stop asking her questions when the answers are making you feel worse!*

"Because I wouldn't do what he wanted anymore and I was going to tell The Brothers what he was up to."

Clifford was going to have to steer this conversation elsewhere, because it all sounded decidedly dodgy, and the last thing he wanted was to star in a real-life episode of *The Sweeney*—or *Casualty* if his heart gave up on him. He'd loved watching those back in the day, but with his unpredictable ticker and his overactive imagination, he didn't need any extra trauma.

He glanced around in the hope of finding another dog walker around, someone to pass this problem on to, but no one was in sight. He idly wondered how many people had walked past her resting place, oblivious to the fact she'd been lying there asleep. Or *had* someone seen her and assumed she was homeless? Were they stronger people than him and they'd just walked away because they couldn't be bothered? Or maybe it was like he'd thought earlier, her lying in a sleeping bag could have been a trick. You heard about people being stabbed all the time these days, didn't you. People minding their own business, then they suddenly found themselves injured.

"Where do you come from?" he asked. "France, isn't it?"

"Yes, but I live in London. Is that where I am now?"

Perhaps the masked man had driven for quite some time before bringing her here or, what with that whack to the head, she may have passed out on the journey so had no clue how long she'd travelled. "Yes, you're in London. Daffodil Woods." He wasn't going to inform her that bodies had been found buried here, those poor women from abroad.

Oh God, she's French. Is she another one of them? One of those refugees?

Clifford wished he didn't have such a rigid way of doing things. If he could allow himself to deviate from his daily routine, he might not have come here today and someone else would be dealing with this. But routine kept him sane. Years ago he would have been so concerned for her, but these days that concern had to centre around himself and Fidel, who would be all alone should something happen to him. Mind you, despite this need of his to keep to himself, Clifford had asked one of the neighbours to keep an eye out every day to see if he went out on his walks with the dog—at least then if he had a heart attack and died, Fidel would be rescued at some point.

He looked at his car, even more desperate to drive away.

To take his mind off that thought, he stared down the track that led to the main road and waited for the sight of another car coming this way. As she didn't speak anymore, he assumed she either had nothing to say or she didn't want to talk, and that was okay, it suited him nicely.

Inevitably, someone else arrived, and at the sound of their footsteps, Clifford turned to stare behind Leanora at a man with a prancing white toy poodle at his side. At the sight of Leanora's expression changing—she must have heard the footsteps—Clifford raised his hand to let her know she didn't need to be alarmed, that she was still safe, and then the poodle came along to make friends with Fidel.

"Don't come any closer," Clifford said to the man. "This poor woman has been through a dreadful ordeal, and I don't want either of us to make it worse. The Brothers have been informed."

"Oh, blimey," the man said, and he looked at his watch.

So it isn't just me who doesn't want to be involved. He's probably got to get to work and doesn't want to hang about.

Or bloody hell, is he her accomplice?

Clifford backed away, moving nearer to his car.

The man raised a hand himself. "Can I just…get in my car. I don't want to cause any trouble. Come on, pup."

He clicked his fingers and strode past Leanora. He didn't look at her, nor at Clifford. Maybe he thought Clifford was the one to fear, that there was some weird dynamic going on between him and Leanora, where she didn't call out for help. The stranger headed for his car, the poodle bunny-rabbiting along behind him, and when he opened the back door of a red saloon, the dog waited to be placed inside. He drove off, not once glancing their way.

"There will be others coming along at some point," Clifford said, and even though he didn't want any blood on his seats, he suggested, "so maybe it's best if you go and sit in my car?"

She shook her head.

Clifford resumed his perusal of the near distance, relieved to see a white van trundling up the track past Poodle Man's car. "Ah, I think your saviours are here. To me, Fidel." He clicked his thumb and finger.

It was clear the dog didn't want to leave her, but nevertheless, Fidel got up and loped over, sitting next to Clifford who now had the chance to put on his lead and ensure he didn't escape again. The van parked close to Leanora, and two big men got out, thick beards, longish hair, and pairs of black-framed glasses. Neither of them were in the infamous grey suits with red ties, and neither of them looked like any descriptions Clifford had ever been given about the twins, mainly from Ida who'd put them on some kind of hero pedestal.

"Hang on a moment," Clifford said, sounding braver than he felt—while he hadn't wanted to be involved in this, he was, so he had some kind of duty of care towards Leanora, as one human being to another. Besides, Ida would want him to help her instead of whinging to himself about how inconvenient this was. "Who are you, because you're not The Brothers."

"I assure you, we are," one of them said and stared down at Leanora. "Come on, love."

She glanced across at Clifford. "It's them, it's okay, and thank you for your help." She got up and huddled inside that ghastly sleeping bag, shuffling off with the other man who'd so far stood back and looked menacing.

The first one stuck a hand in the pocket of his ugly red-and-black-checked jacket. Clifford panicked, thinking he was bringing out a weapon, but all that came towards him was a thick envelope.

"For your help," The Brother said, then he walked off and got in the back of the van.

Clifford stared through the windscreen at Leanora in the passenger seat who held up both hands in a wave. He nodded back in return, sufficiently perturbed enough by the morning's events to put Fidel in the car. He'd take him to one of those fields specifically for walking dogs. He'd have to pay to use it, but it was better than staying here and possibly bumping into a killer.

Fidel got in, clearly confused as to why he wasn't currently haring around through the trees, and Clifford clipped him onto the doggy seat belt to keep him safe. He got in the driver's side and waited for the van to leave, but the driver flashed his headlights at him, indicating that Clifford should go first.

Were they thinking of following him home?

Did it matter if they were?

No, Clifford hadn't done anything wrong, he'd done a good deed.

He drove away, shaking, relieved when at the bottom of the track, they turned left and he turned right. Finally, the tightness in his chest lessened, and he felt able to go about his day, but he'd never forget the most bizarre half an hour that had just occurred and how it had proved to him what a selfish, selfish man he'd become.

Ida would say he ought to be ashamed of himself.

Chapter Thirteen

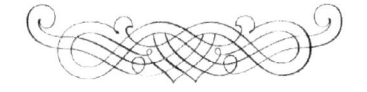

George couldn't believe what he'd heard. On the journey to The Angel, Leanora had shared her story. Once upon a time he would have been royally annoyed at her for even considering helping those balaclava blokes by storing those boxes, but she made a fair point about one of them waving a shotgun around, and he supposed she'd been scared enough to just do as she been told and hope that eventually, they'd find someone else, a new location, and leave her alone.

When she'd got the courage up to finally message George and Greg, some bloke had phoned her, issuing threats, and she'd lied to him, saying the twins would be with her shortly and that he needed to come and pick up the boxes. A bit of a stupid thing to say, to be honest, because the boxes being removed meant any evidence went along with them, but then she'd said the man had emptied them and left them behind, so she'd popped them in the storeroom. He hadn't had gloves on, which was handy.

Colin had responded last night regarding the ferries and planes, calling in a couple of favours to get information, and Leanora's passport hadn't been used. George had kicked himself again for not going through her cupboards and drawers to check if the passport was in the flat; his mind had gone into overdrive, because if she hadn't gone to France, then there was a high chance she might have been abducted by this Tommy fella.

Or, now she'd mentioned them, two men in balaclavas and one in a clown mask.

When she'd got to the bit about Clown Man trying to kill her, George had worked out she was surplus to requirements in whatever game those three were playing. Then again, it wasn't 'whatever game', was it, because it was all about bricks of coke, so the rules were obvious, and she'd broken them.

She'd mentioned stabbing through the clown mask, although she wasn't sure if the scissors she'd used had cut him. Then she'd shown photos of the van number plate, which George would send to their PI to see if it was real. She'd ended on the part where she'd been left in the woods.

Seeing as Greg had pulled down the side of the pub and parked, George reckoned they could cut the conversation here and continue it inside. He'd already messaged ahead to let Lisa know they needed to use Debbie's old room in the parlour and that a couple of strong drinks needed to be on hand for when they arrived.

"Let's get you indoors." George jumped out the back of the van and walked round to the passenger side, opening the door and holding out his arm for Leanora to take it.

She seemed relieved to have got everything off her chest, and it was also likely that as George hadn't barked at her or told her off for engaging with those three men in nefarious activities, then she was off the hook for getting in any trouble. There had been so many times in the past where the same scenario had presented itself over and over. People thought they could handle the situations they'd found themselves in, but time and again they'd had to turn to The Brothers for help when, if they'd just done that in the first place, they wouldn't have even gone through any trauma.

There was no telling some people.

Lisa opened up and ushered them into the private room. Two sofas sat opposite each other, and at the end of both, side tables, one with a bottle of gin and some tonic water, the other with a teapot and three cups. When they were all inside and Lisa had gone, Leanora sitting beside Greg, George poured her a double gin, which she took gratefully, sipping it. He made her a cup of tea as well, letting the silence of this safe room comfort her, giving her time to process what she'd been through.

Which was a lot.

George pointed to her tea and then sat on the other sofa.

They remained in quiet contemplation for about two minutes, George mentally getting his ducks in a row and working out which questions he ought to ask her first. He had a million of them, but only a handful were actually important, and he had to remember she'd been through shit and didn't need him piling more on top. It would be difficult to keep himself in check when all he wanted to do was batter the fuck out of whoever the masked men were, but he'd have to maintain some sense of calm while in her company. If Tommy was nothing to do with it, then George had no idea how they were going to discover the identities of the other men.

It dawned on him then that he could get hold of Bennett or John and ask them to check the CCTV outside the café, see if anyone had loitered about or looked suspicious in the past few days. If visual activity could be discovered out the back on stored footage, that would be even better. Not only would they have the chance to see where the balaclava men had gone after they'd been to the café but also the drug customers.

He fired off a message into the CCTV WhatsApp group, then, bored of waiting for Leanora to speak, decided to get the ball rolling again. All this sitting around contemplating was doing his nut in.

"Who's your ex-boyfriend?"

"Tommy Coda."

"Do you think this could have anything to do with him?"

"Tommy?" She let out a dry laugh. "He likes to be in control and he was upset when I finished with him, but no, I don't think he's capable of doing something like this. He has a manipulative side, and I could see damn well what he was trying to do in wearing me down so he could call all the shots. He didn't show me any signs when I was packing my things that he was angry, more that he was confused as to how I'd guessed what he was doing to me."

"Right, and where is his house?"

She told him, and it was opposite the river, one of those swanky places that cost a fair few quid.

"What does he do for a living in order to afford that?"

"He's a car salesman."

As the name didn't ring a bell, especially for protection money purposes, George asked, "Where's his business located?"

"South London."

"That's probably why we've never heard of him, even though he lives in the East End. So as far as you're concerned, he's just a typical narcissist who enjoys controlling his girlfriends after he's lured them in with a bucketload of charm."

"That's about the sum of it."

"So you stored the boxes of drugs and then you helped to sell them to people who came in the middle of the night."

"Yes. I opened the back door. At one point I wanted to give the balaclava men a key so they could let themselves in and deal with things on their own, but they insisted *I* let them in. I didn't know what was being sold, I guessed. We went into my storeroom, and I had to give them carrier bags out of the boxes which were always taped back up again afterwards. Some nights, the balaclava men didn't come and only the customers turned up—these were ones who'd been before."

"It sounds like they wanted you to be more involved than you needed to be. Like you said, you could have just given them a key and let them get on with it. Maybe they took pictures of you selling the product and planned to hold it over you later down the line if ever you went against them."

"And then I did, and look what happened." She lifted a hand to the gash on her forehead that had scabbed over.

"We'll get our doctor to see to that, plus we'll cut those handcuffs off. Also, one of our men will be here soon to take you to a safe house. His name's Will. He'll stay with you until it's okay for you to go back to the café."

"How long will it take? The girl who works for me, Sally, she needs the wages I pay her."

"It's fine, we've sorted that, so there's no rush. Harley's going to find another job in the meantime to make up his wage from the other sandwich place. Actually, we can find him something to do and pay him a few quid instead. He could help the chefs in either of our pubs."

"Thank you. Where will you begin with this?"

"There'll be surveillance on the café, back and front, but it'll come as no surprise to you that we'll be paying Tommy a visit to rule him out."

Or in, whatever the case may be.

Chapter Fourteen

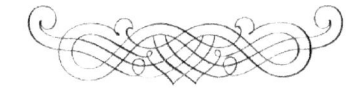

LEANORA ARCHAMBEAU: *Mrs Blanchard has agreed to my offer. I'm coming over on the Channel Tunnel today to see the place for myself. The café looks lovely on the video and exactly what I want, so I don't foresee any problems. Would you like to*

meet for a drink somewhere before I head back?

TommyCoda: That would be great. How quickly do you think the sale will go through?

Leanora Archambeau: A couple of months.

TommyCoda: That's seems so long, even when it isn't really. What will you call the business?

Leanora Archambeau: French Café. I want people to know that French cakes and baguettes are on offer, something different from their norm.

TommyCoda: Once the sale is official, I can put up some posters on the windows if you like, giving people an idea of what's coming. Obviously you could get a designer to create something to your style and send the file over to me so I can get it printed.

LEANORA ARCHAMBEAU: *I can't believe this is happening. I'm so grateful you popped up on that forum.*

TOMMYCODA: *It's been a pleasure to help you. When will you arrive? Do you want me to meet you at the train station? I can hold up a piece of paper with your name on it.*

LEANORA ARCHAMBEAU: *Thank you for the offer, but I'll be all right. I'll be meeting Mrs Blanchard at the café, and then I can meet you for a drink afterwards. I'd prefer a public place.*

TOMMYCODA: *I understand. You don't know me from Adam. Okay, there's a pub down the road, the Blue Dolphin. What time would you like me to be there?*

LEANORA ARCHAMBEAU: *Can I message you later when I know how much time I've got to play with?*

TOMMYCODA: *Of course you can, not a problem.*

LEANORA ARCHAMBEAU: *I really am grateful for everything you've done to help me. I can't believe my dream might be coming true.*

TOMMYCODA: *It's good to have dreams. [smile emoji]*

Tommy stood at the bar in the Blue Dolphin, listening to some old duffer chatting away to the barman, Barry, who was looking after the place for the landlord who'd gone on a little holiday. Tommy wasn't usually nervous about meeting a woman, but this was the biggest scam he'd ever done involving one of them. During the time between now and Leanora moving to England, he was going to spend as much time talking to her on private message as he could. A wacky idea had come into his head earlier, and he hadn't digested it properly yet. He'd poked around on her profile to see her pictures, and she wasn't ugly, so that wasn't an issue, but was it nuts of him to think he could get her to live with him instead of the flat above the café so she never discovered what was going on downstairs in the middle of the night? He could get a set of keys cut, and she'd be none the wiser.

Yes, it was definitely nuts, because she'd likely spot the drug boxes.

Anyway, he found her attractive, and it'd been a long time since he'd been with a woman, so maybe he ought to give her a go. Who knew, he might actually end up caring for her. Mum had been telling him for a while that she wanted him to be happy and settled in a relationship, but he wouldn't necessarily want her to know he was with someone. She'd be a pest and want to set up girl dates with her, like getting their nails and hair done together. Tommy wasn't ready to share anybody like that, not yet.

A cold blast of air alerted him to the door opening, and he turned to see who'd come in. And there she was, Leanora Archambeau, stunning as fuck and just his type. She was prettier in the flesh, and her smile of relief upon seeing him made her even more beautiful. He gave her a smile back and stepped forward with a hand out to shake hers.

"Mr Coda," she said, her French accent strong.

He reckoned he could fall in love with her.

"Miss Archambeau. What would you like to drink?"

"Just a Coke, please. I have a taxi booked in an hour to take me back to the station."

He led her to a table by the bar and left her to settle into her seat while he ordered the drinks. He returned to the table and passed her Coke over, oddly shaken when her fingertips brushed his hand. He'd never been that bothered by women before, none of this 'electricity between them' nonsense, but with her? He could see himself getting pretty attached if he allowed it.

"So what did you think of the café in person?" he asked.

"It's exactly what I wanted, and I let my lawyer know to go ahead with things. I don't want to lose the place now I've seen it, and Mrs Blanchard is eager to be moving to Australia. So hopefully with neither of us wanting to have anything getting in our way, it should all go through quickly."

"That's brilliant. So you're going back to France this evening then?"

She nodded. "I need to work out when to close my current café in Lille."

"What's it like there?"

"Beautiful, but it holds too many sad memories for me now. It's time to move on." She told him about a

restaurant, her favourite one, where she usually had Jupiter lager, Flemish stew, and crème brûleé afterwards. She seemed far away, nostalgic, as though she'd already left her homeland behind. Maybe it was just hitting her now, that it would only be a memory in the future, unless she popped back for a visit. "I miss it already." She laughed.

"That's the beauty of the Tunnel. You can get on the train and be in Lille in under an hour and a half. I'm sure your friends will be pleased to see you when you pop back for visits."

"I don't have any. I told you, it's just me now."

This woman was sounding better by the minute. No family, no friends, no one to give a shit how he treated her. He could mould her to his way of thinking, create the perfect partner. She seemed malleable.

They talked for another forty minutes, then she announced she'd wait outside for her taxi. Tommy would have offered to take her to the station in his van, but it wasn't exactly posh and he didn't want her to get the wrong impression—that he didn't have any money when he did. Besides, he didn't want to push it. He was lucky she'd agreed to meet him for a drink as it was, considering they were basically strangers, so it was best he went down the softly-softly route and got to know her online. Get her to trust him even more.

Get her to think it was the best idea on the planet for her to move into his house rather than the flat above the café.

The problem was, he could easily see himself falling for her, and that was one spanner in the works he hadn't envisaged. Being in love shifted your focus. You didn't see things as clearly as before. He'd have to be on his guard, ensure he didn't fuck up and allow her to skew his emotions.

Out on the pavement, she kissed him on both cheeks then dived into the back of the taxi as though embarrassed to have been so forward. He acted stunned, tentatively smiling at her through the window and raising a hand as the cab pulled away. A message tone went off in his pocket, and he took the phone out to see who'd contacted him.

It was her. A love heart emoji.

Well, fucking hell!

Chapter Fifteen

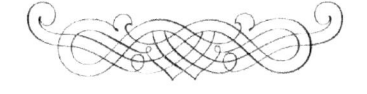

Tommy hadn't slept very well. He supposed that shouldn't have been a surprise, considering he'd killed someone last night, but what had actually kept him awake was the annoyance of having to go to the lock-up just after midnight to speak to the two sets of customers who'd been redirected nearby in order to buy drugs. As per Tommy's earlier instruction via messages, he'd told them to go to a certain tree so the Unidenticals could meet them, pop the blindfolds on, and take them to the lock-up. It was no different to how things had worked when they'd used the café, so the customers kicking off had made no sense whatsoever.

Neither of them had believed it wasn't a setup until Tommy had hidden his car around the corner then strutted up in his clown mask and spoken to them. As soon as they'd heard his voice and he'd let them know that the café was now completely out of bounds and the owner had been *dealt* with, the customers had backed off with their aggression towards Noel and Joel.

Tommy reckoned it had been a dent to their ego that they'd had to get *him* to calm things down when usually, their well-thought-out words of warning did the trick. Noel had said he'd been ready to kick the shit out of the buyers, and the level of disrespect when they'd worked together fine previously was something he wasn't prepared to tolerate in the future. He'd also muttered, "I don't get paid enough for this shit and I'm sick of it." The customers had clearly been spooked by something, possibly the change of location at short notice, despite Tommy messaging them about it.

Thankfully, it had all been smoothed over and he'd gone back home to bed. A bed where he'd tossed and turned for the majority of the night, finally getting up at five a.m. to sling some coffee down his throat and stare across the road at the Thames, wondering what fresh hell today would bring. He'd gone back to sleep at seven for a long nap which had made him feel worse, and now, showered and dressed with a chunk of the morning gone, he was about to go to work, show his face, dish out a few instructions, and then return here to have a lazy afternoon on the sofa.

The perks of being the boss.

The jarring ring of the doorbell got on his last nerve. At this time of the morning it was likely to be the chirpy postwoman who always lingered by telling some banal story he had no interest in. He swore she fancied him, although she was too old for his tastes, and it did nothing for his ego to have some hanger-on of about fifty eyeing him up.

He moved away from the window to go and check the security camera monitor on the wall in the hallway. If it was her, he'd ignore her. She could put a card through the door to tell him a parcel or whatever had been left with a neighbour or returned to the sorting office.

He all but jumped a mile at the figures on the screen. What the fuck were *they* doing here? Shit, Tommy should have realised they'd be round once they'd discovered Leanora wasn't at the café when they'd gone to meet with her. It hadn't taken them long to discover his link to her. But she could have written his name down on something in the flat, a diary, whatever, or they had people in their pocket who'd been willing to talk and say he'd had Leanora living with him at one time. The silly cow must have told people his address, even though he'd asked her not to. He'd asked her to keep all her post going to the café.

He was going to have to open the door and speak to them, putting it off was pointless, but he wished he'd been given more time to compose himself.

Saying that, during the wakeful hours of last night, he'd gone over his alibi, and although it was a weak one, him staying home to watch Netflix alone, unless they had someone on their books in his street who would have seen him leaving in the van, then who was to know *what* he'd been up to?

Conscious he'd already spent too much time looking at the monitor when they could probably see his shadow from outside through the frosted glass in the front door, he turned the screen off, straightened his tie, and threw his shoulders back as he strutted down the hallway. He flung the door open and smiled as though he didn't know who they were.

"Jehovah's Witness?" he asked brightly.

"Do we fucking look like we're selling God, you absolute bellend?" one of them barked. "Step the fuck back."

"Um, no, sorry, I'm not letting you in. I don't know who you are…" Tommy had to hide his smirk at the insult, especially because the twin who'd spoken to him looked completely affronted.

"George," the upset one said, pointing at himself, and then, jerking a thumb in his brother's direction, "Greg. Wilkes. The Brothers. Leaders of the Cardigan Estate. Is that enough hints for you?"

"That's all very well you *saying* who you are, but as I've never clapped eyes on you before, how am I supposed to know?"

Going by the glare of pure hatred coming from George, Tommy guessed the pair of them had heard that excuse before. He really was pushing it, behaving this way, so he decided to back down before everything went tits up.

He held both hands up. "Okay, okay, but you can't be too careful these days, can you. Come through to the kitchen."

Keep playing it cool…

He got on with sorting coffee from his posh barista machine without asking if they wanted one. Instead, he raised an eyebrow at both of them in turn and, receiving nods, took three cups out of the cupboard.

"Is this about protection money?" he enquired casually, "because my business is situated south of the river so…"

"Nope, nothing to do with that."

George stood far too close, but Tommy ignored it as if his arsehole wasn't spasming. Except it was. And he didn't like it.

"So what's up then?" He passed a coffee to George. "Milk and cream is in the fridge, sugar's over there on the drinks' station." He flapped a hand towards a narrow display cupboard on wheels.

George went over there. "Leanora Archambeau. Tell me about her."

To hide his alarm, Tommy shrugged, sorting Greg's coffee. "There's not much to tell when all's said and done. I got chatting to her online, some forum or other regarding business properties. She wanted to know if there were any premises in London suitable for a café. I told her about one, and she said she'd take a look. We kept chatting after, got close over a few weeks, and in the end I fell for her. She moved into my place, then things went wrong. She left, lives above the café now, and that's the end of it."

Greg took the offered coffee. "*Is* it the end of it, though?"

"What do you mean?"

"You've been seen standing on the other side of the road to the café, you pervy fucking wanker."

Who told them that?

Tommy reared his head back and widened his eyes. "I beg your pardon?"

"You heard," George said.

"I've stood over the road, yes, but I'm not a pervert."

"Have you been watching her or something?" George poured sugar into his cup from a glass container with a silver spout.

"Just to check that she's okay," Tommy said.

"So why make out you didn't do it?" Greg asked. "I mean, that's lying, and we don't like being lied to. When we are, it tends to make my brother twitchy. Like, he'll slash your face to bits without even thinking twice."

Fucking hell, these two are nutters.

"Err, it wasn't exactly lying," Tommy said. "It's just I knew how it'd look if I admitted to it. What's she done, told you some bullshit about me?"

Greg went over to the station to put sweetener in his cup. "Someone else has."

"Who?" Tommy asked. He'd be arsey as fuck if it was the Unidenticals, but then if they'd spoken to the twins about him… Actually, why *would* they? There was no reason for those four to be anywhere near each other, he was just getting paranoid.

"We don't reveal our sources," George said. "And people like you who expect us to get right on my nerves, just so you know."

The sledgehammer threats were getting on Tommy's nellies, but it wasn't like he could do anything about them, considering who shared his kitchen. "What do you need to know about her for anyway?"

"She seems to have gone missing," George said.

"Seems?" Tommy scoffed. "Either she has or she hasn't."

"Word has it she's gone back to France."

Tommy didn't want to have to say this, but in order to appear trustworthy, he'd have to. "That's bollocks, she wouldn't go there. There was nothing for her, which was why she came here in the first place." Hopefully, that would get suspicion off him.

"Whereabouts is she from?"

"Lille." He wasn't sure why they needed to know that, but again, he wasn't about to ask. He had a feeling if he prodded George too much he'd end up with a fist in his face.

"When did you last see her?" Greg asked.

"God knows."

"That's all right," George said, "we have someone looking through hours of CCTV down the street where the café is. We'll soon know exactly when you were there."

Tommy's stomach rolled over. They were going to know he'd gone there recently. Were there cameras at the back that he wasn't aware of? He'd scoped the place out, obviously, but he supposed he could have missed something. Thank God he'd worn a clown mask during every night visit.

"It doesn't bother you then, about the CCTV?" George parked his arse on a chair at the table.

"Why would it?" Tommy feigned disinterest. "If I *have* been there recently and I've forgotten, then it's because I've been a little busy and my mind's been elsewhere."

George stared at him. "On what?"

Tommy was going to have to lie. "I've been thinking of expanding my business, setting up a garage in the East End, which is why I was on that online forum."

"Don't forget to get in contact with us if that happens," George reminded him unnecessarily.

"I don't shirk my responsibilities when it comes to paying protection money, thank you."

That had sounded a bit pissed off, and Tommy had to remind himself whose company he was keeping.

"No need to be snarky," George warned.

Greg also sat at the table, so Tommy made himself a coffee, weirded out by how they didn't speak and just glared at him as if they knew he'd done something wrong. Or that could be his guilty conscience talking—not that he felt guilty for killing the silly bitch, she deserved everything that had come her way.

Someone might have found her by now, even though he'd covered the sleeping bag with leaves. There could be police up there and all sorts, one of those white tents and pigs in overalls, like he'd seen on *Vera*. It was a shame he had no excuse to go up there so he could have a nose—unless he asked his mum if he could borrow her dog. But wasn't that what the police would be looking for, someone returning to the scene of the crime?

"What are you thinking about?" George asked, startling him out of his head and back into the present.

"My relationship with Leanora," Tommy fibbed. "A shame it ended and whatever."

"What was her reason for moving out?" Greg eyed him funny.

Is this a trick question? "She said I was too controlling. And I was. Not because I wanted to manipulate everything, but I don't like not knowing what's going on, I kind of need an itinerary of sorts, and she took it that I was spying on everything she did at all times of the day."

"I understand that," George said, "I tend to be controlling myself."

Again, they sat quietly, so Tommy leaned against the worktop, sipped his coffee, and tried to think of something to say that wouldn't make him look a dickhead. Nothing sprang to mind, so it was probably better that he kept his mouth shut. Whenever he was intimidating someone, if they babbled it was a sure sign they were shitting bricks and guilty of something. He'd make sure he remained composed.

George and Greg stood at the same time as though they had some preconceived signal that indicated when they should leave. They walked over and placed their cups on the worktop next to the sink.

"Very good coffee," George said. "I'm a bit partial to my Tassimo, but this stuff was even nicer. Mind if I take a picture of your machine? I might well get one myself."

Tommy gestured for him to do what he liked, he just wanted the pair of them out of his house. He was going to ditch going to the car showroom; he'd sent an email to Lionel to let him know he wasn't coming in. Sod it, he was going to use Mum's dog and see what he could get away with in Daffodil Woods. He had a fake beard and some glasses he could put on, plus that black wig in his wardrobe. He could give a false name if the police were up there and asked him questions. He couldn't stand not knowing whether the body had been discovered yet.

"Is there an actual reason you were asking me about Leanora?" Tommy asked as he showed them out.

The twins turned on the doorstep to face him.

"You must have the memory of a goldfish," George said, "because I'm sure I mentioned the fact that she'd gone missing, possibly back to France. As I recall, you told me that was bollocks."

"Oh yeah. Sorry I wasn't much help. I can try ringing her if you want?" Tommy cursed his big mouth. Her phone was in the sideboard in his living room. He couldn't remember if he'd turned it off or not, but he must have done, because he wouldn't have wanted any of the masts to pick up its location.

"No thank you," George said.

If they were looking into her disappearance, why weren't they taking all the help they could get?

George studied him. "What's that on your face?"

Tommy frowned. "What do you mean?"

"That cut on your cheek."

Fuck. Fuck! "Oh, that. I nicked it when I was shaving this morning."

"That's a big nick."

"Yeah, I'm well clumsy."

"So you say."

The Brothers walked away and got into a small white van parked behind Tommy's. He'd swear blind they usually swanned about in a BMW, but what did he know? He turned and went inside, closing the door, then rushed into the living room to check her phone. It was definitely off, but he was going to have to get rid of it. Having it in his house was giving him too much anxiety.

He went upstairs and got changed into clothes appropriate for walking a dog.

Let's go and see what's what.

Chapter Sixteen

Tommy left his van at his mum's house, the number plate doctored, and took her car because of the dog guard in it. He drove her mutt, Ralph, in the direction of Daffodil Woods, pausing in a lay-by to change a couple of letters on Mum's number plate. He set off again towards the right-hand track that led to the woods and frowned. He'd expected to see at least one police officer in a yellow high-vis jacket, plus a cordon stopping people from going in, but no one stood there.

What the fuck was going on?

He turned onto the track and peered ahead at the car park at the top of the incline. Ralph whined; he must know where they were going. Maybe Mum brought him up here often. The noise grated on Tommy's nerves; he didn't do whingy dogs. He parked beside a row of other cars, glancing across to where the walking tracks started. Three sprouted off in different directions; last night he'd driven his van down the farthest one on the right.

He stuck the beard and glasses on and stuffed his hair inside a black beanie hat. In his haste to get here, he'd forgotten to take the bloody wig out of the wardrobe, but he wasn't going to beat himself up about it now. Out of the car, he rounded it to the boot and let Ralph out. The black-and-white collie sat patiently while Tommy unclipped the lead, and then they were off. The absence of police cars unsettled him, but maybe they were down the track where he'd left the body.

The farther he walked, the more he realised nothing was going on here. He turned into the clearing and strode to the hidden area where he'd dumped the bitch.

His body went cold, his legs almost giving way.

She wasn't there.

Jesus Christ, had she still been alive when he'd left her? Had she got up and fucked off? Was that why the twins had paid him a visit? Did they know damn well what had happened to her and they'd questioned him to try to find out if it had been him? People always suspected the ex. The not knowing all the details coiled his guts and sent his heart tickering too fast.

He followed the dog out of the hidey-hole, gesturing to let Ralph know he could have a run about. It would give Tommy time to think, get his fear to back off. Ralph understood the message but instead of stretching his legs along the track, he shot off into a nearby bush, pissing Tommy off because he knew from experience it would take ages to get the animal back out if Ralph was of a mind to play silly buggers. He tromped over, anger surging, and ended up circling the bush and getting down on his hands and knees to try and find the dog inside. The dampness from the ground seeped through his trousers, and he wanted to scream.

"Get out, you stupid little bastard," he shouted, the urge to leave Ralph there too strong for words. He should never have come, he shouldn't have been so cocky to think that he could swan around here and get away with it if the police were in the vicinity. As it was, he'd turned up and no fucker was here, and he had the massive dilemma of where the hell Leanora had gone.

He didn't think fate would be on his side to the point that some other weirdo had picked her dead body up inside that sleeping bag and carried her away. What were the odds of that happening? Bloody low. There was no way other people wouldn't have come along here yet either, dog walkers or joggers, so if she hadn't been removed by someone else, and she hadn't got up by herself, then where the hell was she?

Ralph crawled out from under the bush then legged it down the track. Tommy got up and chased after him, slipping on the mud and almost going arse over tit.

"I swear to God, if you don't come back…"

Ralph didn't give a toss about the warning and kept running. Tommy stopped, too irate to continue the chase. Tommy leaned against a tree and pulled at the sides of his beanie to redirect his rage, convinced now that Leanora had somehow stayed alive. But how could she have survived him suffocating her?

There was no way. She'd been limp and everything when he'd put her in the sleeping bag, and he'd waited for ages in the clearing to watch and see whether she'd get up.

Someone *must* have found her.

Ralph came bounding back and headed the way they'd come. The stupid animal waited for him by the car, and Tommy made his way towards him. Someone else came out of one of the other walkways, a woman with a silver Great Dane.

"Morning," Tommy said, as though he hadn't just been looking for the bird he'd murdered. "Nice day for it."

What did you draw attention to yourself for?

She nodded, gave a tight smile, and trotted off in her muddy trainers, letting her dog into the back of a burgundy Range Rover, then driving off down the track. For a moment Tommy forgot he had a disguise on, and his stomach muscles clenched, but he caught sight of his reflection in a car window as he passed it, and his anxiety eased—if she was ever asked about anyone up here, she wouldn't be able to give his real description.

Putting Ralph in the back of the car, then taking the tape off the number plate, he got in the driver's seat and sat there for a moment, staring down the track. Vehicles drove past on the road, but none of them turned to come up here.

What was he supposed to do now? Scour the whole woods in search of her? If she wasn't here, how could he find out where she was without it looking obvious he was trying to discover whether she was alive or dead? Maybe, because the twins had been to his house, he could make out he was helping them in locating her. Would that annoy them if they heard about it, though? Would they see it as him stepping on their toes if he went around asking questions? He didn't fancy another visit, but maybe he'd get one anyway if they were playing games with him and somehow Leanora had managed to get hold of them to pick her up.

How? I have her phone.

He imagined her standing by the road, the sleeping bag wrapped around her, waving to passing motorists. Pleading for help and no one stopping. What would he have done in her position? Walked and walked until he found humanity. But she might have suffered from that head injury and fallen into a ditch. She could be dead, slowly rotting.

Or she could be alive.

The idea of that sent a sluice of ice through his veins. He could start by ringing hospitals and asking if anyone had come in. She needed her forehead looking at, but it would seem odd if he phoned up to see how she was. They probably wouldn't tell him anything anyway, those bloody nurses were a secretive lot.

He gunned the engine and drove away, plotting his next move. By the time he got to Mum's he had everything in order. He took the dog into the kitchen, glad to hand over the responsibility of the naughty little sod.

"What the fucking hell have you got on your *face*?" Mum gawped at him.

Shit, he'd forgotten to take off the disguise. That was all he needed, twenty questions. "If you must know, I was following someone in the woods."

Mum frowned. "What the bloody hell *for*? I hope you haven't turned into one of them weirdos."

He was going to have to lie again. It was becoming a bit of a habit. "Look, a customer owes me finance payments on a car, and I wanted to have a word with him where he couldn't fob me off. He's been ignoring my phone calls and emails. I know he takes his dog to the woods at the same time every week on the same day because he said so when he was buying the car, so I caught up with him and let him know that if he didn't pay there'd be trouble."

Had that sounded plausible? By the way Mum stared at him, he didn't think so.

"So you decided to put on a beard and glasses in order to speak to someone who knows you without a beard and glasses. And you think I'm going to believe that? Because you know I can always tell when you're lying. Are you up to no good?"

"It's best you don't know," he said, "now leave it at that."

He shouldn't have said that. It was only going to make her worse. She'd turn into Poirot in a minute.

"How can I leave it at that when you said something that sounds like you *are* up to no good?" She leaned against a cupboard and folded her arms. "What kind of mess have you got yourself into? Talking about it might make you find a solution. You said some bloke owes you for finance, but I'm sorry, that's a load of old cobblers."

"I'm telling you now, Mum, this isn't something I can talk about, nor is it anything you'd want to hear."

"You could murder someone and I'd still want to hear about it," she said.

That wasn't a new thing. She'd said it often, that no matter what he did, even committing murder, he would always be her son and she would always stand by him. But was that something people just *said* in order to get across the depth of their love? Would it be completely different in real life if he confessed that he had intended to, and thought he had, killed a woman, but when he'd gone back to check on her this morning she had disappeared? Could he stand seeing his mother's face crumple in that awful expression of disappointment he'd spent a lifetime striving to avoid? Could he stand to hear her crying and at the same time telling him what he'd done was bad but she loved him anyway, and may God forgive her for it?

"Would you really, though?" he asked.

"Of course I bloody would!"

"Okay then, I killed someone."

She threw her head back and laughed, and it was so, so clear she didn't believe him. "Pull the other one."

"No, Mum, I killed someone."

She sobered pretty quickly, blinking, maybe to stop her eyes from filling, or maybe she was in shock. She lifted one hand to twist her bottom lip, shifting her attention away from him to the floor. He imagined the fight-or-flight response inside her, or maybe she was in freeze mode. Had adrenaline flounced through her body and sent her legs cold? Was she imagining all the implications of what he'd said—the police knocking on her door to ask her about her son (would she lie to them and say he was a good boy who'd never heard to fly?); him being arrested; her standing there in court, supporting him no matter what, no matter that other members in the gallery gave her filthy looks and said cruel things because she'd stood by her child.

"Have you really?" she asked. "Really-really?"

He nodded.

"And did you mean to?"

He nodded again.

"Fuck…" She straightened her shoulders and walked over to the table, lowering to a chair and splaying her palms either side of a wicker place mat.

He recognised the look, how she was working out the options; he'd seen her doing it many a time as she'd bought him up, when red letters had come about the non-payment of rent and her trying to work out how she was going to pay it — or any bill for that matter. She'd always dug them out of holes in the past, and he could see she was trying to do that again now.

It humbled him how much she loved him, how it appeared she was going to cover up for him regardless of the danger it would put her in. Or maybe that was just his interpretation. She might be willing to give him suggestions but may also phone the police and report him. She might love him wholeheartedly, but she'd brought him up to obey the law.

Clearly, he hadn't listened.

"What happened?" she asked.

"I was seeing this woman…" He held his hand up to stop her from commenting. "She was doing something for me, even though she didn't know it was for me per se. Anyway, she basically threatened to blow the operation wide open, and I lost the plot."

"What operation?"

Should he lie again? Tell her it had something to do with the car showroom? Or maybe it was better to confess everything. He already felt less tension in his shoulders from saying stuff out loud—or saying part of it anyway. The question was, should he fully unburden himself on this subject, to his mother, effectively removing the weight from his shoulders and plonking it on hers? In other circumstances, she'd have said plonk away, but with something of this magnitude, he wasn't sure she ought to know the ins and outs. She had no clue about the drugs racket. If he was going to tell her about the murder, then he was going to have to tell her about that, too, a double whammy that her son wasn't who she'd thought he was.

Could he crush her like that?

"Listen, Mum, there's shit about me you don't know. My life isn't what you think. I'm not respectable Tommy Coda who runs a car showroom. Or I'm not just him. There's another side, and I got into that life from growing up skint."

She scowled. "Is this the bit where you tell me it's my fault?"

"No, it's the bit where I tell you your circumstances spurred me on to make sure you, we, never go without again." He gestured to the kitchen. He didn't want to remind her he'd bought this place for her, cleared her debts, and gave her enough cash on the weekly so she could get her hair and nails done and go out for a few lunches with her mates. Once he told her what else he did for a living, she'd know that cash was dirty money, she'd know she'd inadvertently played a part in breaking the law. Her home and everything in it had been purchased with money earned by him engaging in crime.

She was probably going to give him a right bollocking.

"Whatever it is, son, I'm listening."

Selfish or not, he took the plunge and told her the lot. By the time he'd finished, tears rolled down her face, but she didn't do any noisy crying like she had in the darkest times of his childhood. Maybe this scenario was *too* dark, so fucking dark that she couldn't even summon up a sob.

"Say something, Mum."

She held a palm up, attempted to speak, but no words came out, and he understood that the gravity of this situation had literally rendered her speechless—or was it emotion preventing her from talking to him, a nasty lump in the throat? Shame enveloped him that he'd brought his mother to this, and although the mercenary part of him, the part that didn't ever want to accept responsibility, chirped that this was *her* fault, she'd pushed for an explanation, he had to concede that he could have kept his mouth shut and he hadn't.

She cleared her throat. Pressed her fingertips onto the table. "For…for…" She cleared her throat again. "For the first time in my life, I actually don't know what to do for the best. This is a bit too big for me to handle. I just need a few seconds to go through what you said in my head so I know where we're at."

We're. So she was taking this problem on as hers. The relief brought tears to Tommy's eyes, a bit of that sting belonging to guilt, too, because she'd wanted him to be a good boy and he'd turned out bad.

He got up and made her a cup of tea, a coffee for himself. While he'd been busy she'd taken a notebook and pen from the sideboard and doodled on it—flowers, a house, clouds, birds. She'd always done that when she'd sat to work out her bills, the idle drawings perhaps giving her a chance to find some clarity in her world of poverty and trying to make ends meet. He placed the cups on one of the mats and wanted to sit next to her so she could cuddle him, so he could get some comfort and she'd prove with that hug that she still loved him, but that was a childlike need and something *she* had to offer, not something he had the right to ask for anymore.

He'd stepped over a line and sensed things were different between them now. Of course they were. He'd been lying to her for years. He'd encouraged her to take his drug money and spend it on herself.

She slapped the pen down beside the pad and folded her hands underneath her armpits. "From the sound of things, you covered your arse pretty well. She didn't know you were the man in the clown mask, the one she was storing the drugs for. The Brothers just came to your house because you're linked to her and they'll be trying to piece her life together to find out why she's gone missing, although them saying she's gone back to France, well, that doesn't say she's missing to me, but whatever. I'm not very happy that you used my car to take Ralph to the woods, but it's done now, and like you said, no coppers were there and neither was she, so I doubt anyone in authority will even be looking at the woods or the roads leading up to it to even spot my car going there."

"I doctored the number plate."

"That's something."

"So what do I do now?"

"You sit tight. Close down the drugs business—sell what's left in the lock-up then call it a day. Stick to your showroom, to being the person I thought you were. If the twins come back again, you answer their questions as though you're nothing but this woman's ex. They could be watching you now, so get those other twins to deal with selling the drugs. That way, you won't be spotted going to the lock-up or having anything to do with dodgy shit."

"But what about her?"

"You either didn't kill her, which is a bloody good thing on one hand because you can't get done for murder, just attempted, or you did kill her and someone else has taken her. There's no way if it was the police that there wouldn't have been coppers up in them woods, there'd have been forensics out and everything, so I'd say you're safe there. Could it have been those other twins who picked her up?"

Tommy hadn't thought about that. "What the fuck would they do *that* for?"

"One of them might have got the jitters in the middle of the night and had thoughts about transfer from their lock-up being on her clothes or body. They could have collected her to dispose of elsewhere. Like in water so any evidence gets washed away."

"I'd have thought they'd have told me, though."

"Maybe you ought to ring them and find out."

Chapter Seventeen

In the end, it took four months for the sale to complete. During that time, Tommy had indeed fallen in love with Leanora, finding it odd that he enjoyed her company so much and looked forward to chatting with her when he'd never had that with another woman before. He supposed that was love, or something resembling it, and that it would only get stronger when she eventually came to London.

Two weeks before the sale had finalised, he'd managed to persuade her to move in with him. Her response had annoyed him a bit, that she'd leave the café flat empty, just in case things didn't work out between them. That told him she wasn't as invested in them as he was, and it pissed him off that he appeared to feel more for her than she did for him. Still, he could make that happen once they were together. He'd buy her flowers, take her out for dinner, whisk her back to Lille whenever she got homesick. He'd be the perfect gentleman so long as she behaved herself.

He'd been overseeing a delivery. Mrs Blanchard had given him a set of keys prior to flying off to Australia yesterday, and Tommy had gone to the café to wait for Leanora's furniture to arrive. She'd sent it from France, and the drivers were carrying the items up to the flat. It unsettled Tommy to know she had somewhere else to live should she ever choose to leave him, but he consoled himself that if he ended things with her then she had somewhere to go immediately. He wouldn't have to have her hanging around, getting on his wick.

Once the drivers had left, he opened up some of the boxes to have a nose inside. He'd asked her if she wanted him to put things away, but she'd said no — she was still hanging on to her privacy despite them getting on like a house on fire and admitting they had feelings for one another. He was going to unpack regardless. This way, if he did it without her knowledge and told her afterwards, he could make out it was done as a surprise. Mind you, he'd leave the suitcases with the clothes inside because they'd be going to his place. She'd already asked him to take them over there for her.

To put her mind at ease, or maybe it was to convince her to live with him, he'd videoed another guided tour to show her his beautiful house. He'd offered her the dream, and she'd bought it, although she was somewhat reticent at times. Guarded. He couldn't work her out. Maybe she didn't want to put all her eggs in one basket with him. After all, they'd met online, had only met once in person in the Blue Dolphin, and although they typed messages to one another and spoke on the phone daily, perhaps she still had reservations. That annoyed him. He'd worked so hard to make her feel at ease. He'd let her think she had a say in how things would go.

He took out the contents of one of the boxes — several photo albums containing pictures of her as a child along with who he assumed were her parents.

Although she'd been a teenager when they'd died, at least she'd had a father in her life. Tommy couldn't remember his ever living with them, and his dad had never taken any responsibility for him once he'd walked out. He had left the van to Tommy, though, so that was something, a gesture that showed he'd maybe thought of his son near the end. It seemed Leanora had the best life ever with her parents, and then in other photo albums her aunt, who was clearly her mother's sister. They looked too alike for her not to be.

He placed the albums in a row on the shelves of a wooden unit that stood between two windows in the living room. He arranged her other furniture, rolling out a rug and placing a coffee table on top, then hung some curtains that he'd taken out of a box.

He finally finished the flat four hours later and did a walkaround video. He was weirdly nervous about uploading it to show her what he'd done in case she lost her temper and thought he was taking over, which he was, but her insistence that she unpacked everything had got on his nerves. He didn't want her to have control so had taken it away from her.

That brought him up short. Mum had told him that his father was the same way, always telling her what to do, and when she didn't do it, he'd got angry. She'd told Tommy never to treat a woman that way, it wasn't fair, but he burned inside at the thought of Leanora making decisions without him knowing about them first.

He uploaded the video and hoped for the best.

> LEANORA ARCHAMBEAU: *Oh my God, I know I said I'd do it all when I got there, but you've really taken a weight off my shoulders. I didn't realise how much I was dreading it until I saw it's all done.*
>
> TOMMYCODA: *Thank goodness you're not angry. I only did it because I know how tired you've been lately, burning the candle at both ends. I wanted to help.*
>
> LEANORA ARCHAMBEAU: *I'm really grateful. I can't wait to see you in the morning.*
>
> TOMMYCODA: *I'll wait at the café like you asked me to.*
>
> LEANORA ARCHAMBEAU: *Thank you.*

Tommy studied their interaction and shook his head. She'd explicitly told him not to interfere with the unpacking, and yet look at how she'd responded. No wonder men couldn't work out where they stood with women when they changed their minds at the drop of a hat.

He sent her a string of love heart emojis and locked up the café, eager to get home and have a shower. On the drive there, he pondered his next steps. He'd give her a month to get settled in his house, then he'd send the Unidenticals to the café to force her to let them use the storage room. He had another brilliant idea. Instead of having to use the alarm at the showroom, because all of the car keys were in a portable safe in the office, he'd just take the safe home with him every evening and bring it back in the mornings. There would be no reason to even set an alarm and no reason for Lionel to check when Tommy had switched it on and off during the night. He expected there would be questions, but he could tell Lionel he'd grown paranoid about burglaries in the area, hence him taking the safe home.

If only the man hadn't been so fucking diligent and nosy, Tommy wouldn't even need the café to sell drugs from. The only reason he wanted to use someone else's property was so his name wasn't linked to it if the police got wind of him dealing, otherwise he'd have rented some shitty little office somewhere and worked from there.

It would all come good in the end.

> LEANORA ARCHAMBEAU: *Shall we go out to dinner tomorrow night to celebrate my first evening in London?*
>
> TOMMYCODA: *That would be lovely. My treat.*
>
> LEANORA ARCHAMBEAU: *I'll buy the champagne then.*
>
> TOMMYCODA: *I look forward to it.*

Tommy had never kissed this woman, but he'd dreamed about it often enough. They'd revealed their feelings for each other, of course they had, otherwise she'd never have agreed to move into his house, but what if they weren't sexually compatible? What if they got on each other's nerves after they'd been living together for a couple of weeks? He supposed it didn't matter so long as the café could be used during the night, but since he'd invested so much time and energy into what he considered a proper relationship, then it would be a shame for it to fall apart.

How would he feel if everything went to shit?

How would he cope, going back to the kind of life he'd led before she'd walked into it? Every day that had passed since he'd answered her query on the forum had been spent talking to her. They'd opened up and told each other about their fears, about everything, which was weird because Tommy never did that with anyone. She'd done something to him. Bewitched him.

It was never supposed to be about love, just using her for the café, her being a scapegoat should anyone ever discover where the place was. He trusted his buyers to wear their eye masks and to not peek at their surroundings until he'd escorted them away from his showroom, walking them back to their vehicles around the corner. They'd never known it was him because he'd always worn a clown mask. He was sick of doing all the hard graft. Couldn't wait to pass it to the Unidenticals. He'd lose a portion of the money by paying them for their time, but it meant he'd get a full night's sleep instead of the broken ones he'd been having ever since he'd started dealing drugs in a big way.

This had *to work.*

Chapter Eighteen

Noel shook his head at the name of the caller on his phone screen. He'd been thinking of ways to put an end to their association with Tommy—things might get a bit hairy if they continued their working relationship. The money he paid them was handy, but the amount they had to do for it was not. More and more appointments were being made with buyers, meaning Noel and Joel had to go out in the middle of the night a few times to accommodate them. This murder shit with Leanora was the final nail in the coffin.

We should never have agreed to help him with that.

He swiped to answer. "What now?"

"I just need a straight and honest answer, all right?" Tommy said.

Noel bristled at his tone. What a prick. "Right, but since when have I never given you an honest answer?"

"True."

"Go on then, what's up?"

"Did you go and collect that body from the woods?"

Noel frowned—*is he for bloody real?* "You fucking what?"

"She wasn't there when I had a look this morning."

"So you thought it was us? What the fuck did you go back for?"

"Dunno."

"The rule is never to go back unless you left something behind. Did you?"

"Only the sleeping bag I put her in."

"And can anything on it be traced back to you?"

"I'm not sure. It's been in the back of my van for ages. I slept in it once, that time when I went to buy some gear and the seller was late."

"The answer was supposed to be no, there's nothing on it, but it sounds like there'll be your DNA. What a fucking imbecile. Look, I've made a decision. Once the drugs in the lock-up have all gone, we're calling it a day."

"I was ringing to say the same myself."

A classic response when someone got in there before you, but Noel couldn't be arsed to say so. "No hard feelings, but now we're talking about some dead bird, it's all a bit *too* illegal, if you know what I mean."

"You didn't seem to mind it being illegal when you sat outside while I killed her."

"To be honest, I didn't think you were going to go through with it."

"You're saying I didn't have the balls? Well, I proved you wrong there, didn't I."

"It's not something to brag about, mate." Noel had noticed that with Tommy, how he got cocky about things he shouldn't. "Back to business. We'd rather you arrange to sell the drugs in one go to lessen the amount of traffic coming our way. It's better that we all distance ourselves from each other now."

"That's why I was ringing, my mum said similar."

Fucking hell, had Tommy gone and told his mother what he'd done? "I hope, if you've launched yourself into confession mode with your old dear, you haven't dropped our names in it."

"Of course not."

"You'd better be telling the truth, otherwise…"

"We're good mates, we go back years, there's no way I'd shit all over you."

Noel would have to be satisfied with that until he knew otherwise. "Okay, I want everything over by two in the morning, so get your arse in gear to sort buyers."

"Is it only because of the murder that you've had a change of heart? I mean, you suggested the lock-up to store the drugs, and you went and collected her from the café for me—you didn't seem to have a problem with it then, but now you do?"

"The twins have been sniffing round the café."

"Yeah, they came to my house to ask about my relationship with her. They think she's gone to France. It all sounds a bit dodgy, because one minute she's missing, and the next minute they know where she's gone. It doesn't make sense."

"All the more reason for us to break contact and go our separate ways. I don't fancy them watching me and my brother, thank you."

"Right, I'll be in contact about the drug sales. Take what I owe you out of the money they hand over. If you don't want us to meet in person for you to pass the cash on to me, feel free to leave it in the compost bin in my back garden—obviously put it in a carrier bag."

"Will do. Stay safe, and if you can't stay safe, keep our names out of it."

Noel ended the call and went in search of Joel. He found him counting money in the kitchen of a flat they rented as office space and a place to doss if they were knackered and couldn't be bothered to go home. This morning they'd taken on a new client who'd paid cash for them to go and beat someone up later tonight—they had to give the target a warning without saying the client's name or what the warning was about. A bit odd, but whatever. That had been arranged for nine o'clock when the target left the Noodle pub—there wasn't any CCTV there, unless you counted the nearby video doorbells, and their attack would undoubtedly draw attention, but no one would know who they were, their trusty balaclavas in place and a stolen car parked around the corner ready for a quick getaway.

"Who was on the phone?" Joel asked.

"Tommy. We're in agreement that we part ways. He's sorting a buyer or buyers out for the early hours, then we can wash our hands of him. He mentioned his mother. I've got a feeling he needed to offload to her if you know what I mean."

Joel shrugged. "Cheryl's all right, she won't cause any trouble."

"You don't think we need to worry? He said he hasn't dropped our names in it with her, but you know what he's like, he can lie his way out of anything and sound convincing."

"We covered our backs. We always wear gloves and balaclavas, we've always got our future safety in mind. We scrubbed that lock-up with bleach. He can tell anyone he likes that we were involved in his shit, but there's no proof."

"There's a little problem, though." Noel braced himself for a possible shit fit. "He dumped her in the woods, right, and for whatever reason decided to go back there this morning."

"*What?*"

"Get this—"

"Oh Jesus Christ, what…"

"She wasn't there."

Joel looked disturbed. Angry. "What a stupid fucking bastard."

"He wanted to know if *we'd* gone and collected her."

"Why the hell would we have done *that*?"

"That's what I thought. So if she wasn't there, then where is she, and who took her?"

"Are you sure he's not fucking you about, making out she was gone when really it was him who took her?"

"Why would he even want to do that, though?"

"Maybe so he could put her somewhere that could be linked to us so we get the blame for killing her."

"I don't see why—"

"To take the heat off himself."

Noel had a little think about that. "He did say The Brothers had been to see him."

"They're going be looking at him—he's probably got someone following him as we speak."

"I know. He didn't say which way round things had happened, but if they spoke to him before he went to the woods…"

"…then he could have been tailed there. We can't be seen to have a link with him."

"We've always got balaclavas on when we meet him, and our number plates are always switched out for every visit, but yeah, I agree with what you're saying. I think he's actually genuine about shielding us because he said to take our cut from the drug money we get later and to put the rest in his compost bin."

"*His* compost bin. At *his* house? A house that could have surveillance outside it? Fuck right off. What if it's a trap? We tell him we're on our way, and someone's waiting for us."

"The twins?"

"Yeah." Joel paused in contemplation. "Fucking weird about that body not being there, though. Did he even kill her? She could have just got up and walked off after he left her there. What if he *has* moved her somewhere we can get done for it?"

"Hmm. He's never shafted us before, but I'm uneasy now. Should we drive past the café and see if anything's going on?"

"We're not going anywhere near it. We'll get tonight's job done at the Noodle, do the drug deals, pop his money somewhere of *our* choosing, then that's the end of it."

Noel nodded. "We'll have to draw some more work in. He paid us a steady chunk every week."

"We know who he bought drugs from. We could approach them ourselves."

"Do we really want the hassle?"

Joel shook his head. "Not really, no." He moved to the worktop to stick the kettle on. "I suppose we just keep our ears to the ground regarding the body."

"Or whether she's still alive."

Noel wasn't fussed whether she was or not. She didn't know who they were so couldn't get them in trouble with the police. But maybe she *had* gone back to France and all the twins wanted to know was why. There might not be anything to worry about at all, but sadly, he had a feeling there was.

Chapter Nineteen

For the first time in her life, Cheryl Coda had the urge to go against her son. Just a small urge, a nudge to do the right thing and save herself from getting the blame for being involved, but how could she dob her own child in to the police when they weren't even sure there was a body? Leanora could be alive, walking around as happy as Larry—well, maybe not happy, she'd likely have a bloody sore throat from having those shoelaces clamped across it, plus a sore head, but she might be alive, and Cheryl planned to find out. What she couldn't get to grips with was the fact that Tommy had done those things. He'd *wanted* to kill that woman. She'd been surplus to requirements, and it was worrying that murder had been Tommy's go-to method of dealing with the issue.

Why have I never seen that side of him before?
Is he one of those psychopaths who can hide it?

She'd never met Leanora, hadn't had the privilege of Tommy bringing his girlfriend round for dinner, which had told her the French woman wasn't The One. She couldn't have been, because Tommy hadn't even told Cheryl he was seeing anyone, that they were living together at his place. He'd kept it a complete secret, which now made sense, considering he'd used her café as the place to store drugs.

Drugs!

Cheryl stormed down the high street, incensed that her boy had turned to such a disgusting way of making money. She understood the reasoning behind it, but it didn't mean she had to like it. It must be a lucrative business for him, and all that cash he'd been handing over to her made sense now, plus paying off her mortgage and debts. He said he'd done that using money from the car showroom, which was doing exceptionally well, earning him a nice living, so really, the extra money generated by the drugs wasn't necessary.

She approached the French Café. A couple of women stood outside, one with a black-and-white polka-dot-patterned shopping trolley, the other with a large paper Primark bag hanging on the crook of her arm. Cheryl glanced at the café, the blinds down, the CLOSED sign facing the street. She imagined what had gone on behind there last night, the fear Leanora must have experienced at the hands of those bloody friends of Tommy's. Had they tormented her with the fact she was going to die? Had she gone with them willingly, through fear, or had she put up a fight?

Was there any way, if it came to it, that Tommy could blame the murder on those two?

She'd have to think on it some more.

She stopped by the ladies and waved her arm towards the building, giving them a proper hard frown. "Oh, is it shut?"

Trolley Lady nodded. "I've not long messaged the mother of the young girl who works here—Sandra, her name is. The mother not the girl. The owner's apparently buggered off to France. Shame, because we liked coming here once a week."

Primark Bag sniffed. "Maybe there was a family emergency back home."

"She didn't have any family," Trolley said. "She told us once, remember?"

"Oh yeah, because I got a bit upset for her, didn't I, that she didn't have anyone at all apart from some bloke she was seeing."

"Who was that?" Cheryl asked, needing to know if it was common knowledge that Tommy had been involved with the woman. It felt a little like an affair with Cheryl being the last to know.

Primark shrugged. "She never said."

Cheryl gave them a smile and continued up the high street, heading for Greggs so it looked like her only interest in the café had been to buy something to eat. She picked up a pack of four sausage rolls and a box of doughnuts, then joined the queue. She kept her ears peeled for anyone talking about the French Café, but the mumbled conversations were more to do with day-to-day life and its struggles than anything. She paid for the food and left the shop, nipping to Superdrug for some shampoo, then she walked past the café again. The two women were gone, so Cheryl paused, for what she didn't know—maybe a faint hope she'd hear movement from within indicating Leanora was alive?

Don't be daft.

She continued on to the car park and drove home, surprised to find Tommy was still there, sitting on the sofa next to Ralph who wasn't allowed on furniture and, going by his guilty look and how he quickly sloped off onto the floor, he bloody well knew it, too.

"I've got some lunch," she said. "The blinds are down at the café, and a couple of women were talking. Someone's mum told her the owner's gone to France, so I think you're safe for now."

Tommy seemed zoned out or lost, she couldn't work out which. As for her own feelings, she'd inspect them later. After the initial shock that her son was a possible murderer, she'd just wanted to fix the problem, press plugs into any of the leaking holes to keep her boy safe from having to go to prison—and herself for knowing about it. If what he'd said was true, the only things that could let him down was his van and the sleeping bag, and while he'd changed the number plate, there was still the issue of him having her in that van if there had been witnesses in the woods. No matter what the number plate was, that van lead would be investigated.

"I'll make us a brew."

She placed the Greggs' bag on the coffee table and went into the kitchen where she could sift through some of the most pressing questions that had now entered her head. If she wasn't careful, this whole scenario could turn into a circle of worry where her mind threw up possibilities that she focused on rather than the positive ways she could ensure her son remained free.

Back in the day, when she'd been an overly anxious single mother in her twenties and thirties, she'd let her life become blighted by imagined instances that had never come true. She'd known they wouldn't, but it hadn't stopped her brain from telling her that everything would go to shit—and always in the worst way possible. She'd go to prison for not paying her bills, when in reality, she could offer a payment plan, and it would be fine, stuff like that.

Over the last twelve or so years, she had learned to be more confident, to brush aside any worries after reading a book called *The Chimp Paradox*, which had taught her how to train the Chimp in her brain—the part that focused on emotions and anxiety and gave her all manner of gyp with its ridiculous, intrusive thoughts. But Tommy's confession had shoved away all of her built-over-the-decades confidence, shooting her back to the days when she'd been uncertain and worried about every little thing. It was as if all the hard work she'd learned from the book had been scrubbed away.

Unless she decided to do something about it and listen to her rational side instead. If she could focus on facts, then it would hopefully shut out the absurd chirping of her Chimp.

Go through things, think logically.

One, the café was closed.

Two, the rumour was that Leanora had gone back to France.

Three, it was obvious the twins would have followed up where she was because she likely paid them protection money and they'd want to know where she was for future payments.

Four, Leanora must have woken up in the woods.

Five, if she hadn't—and Cheryl just couldn't see this happening as it was so unlikely—some weirdo dog walker had found her early doors and taken her body somewhere.

Six, based on number five happening and a weirdo not wanting anyone to know they had a dead body, said body would likely be disposed of at some point, hidden so it wasn't discovered, therefore, Tommy still wouldn't get done for anything.

"If he just keeps his nose clean," she muttered, "then we can come out on the other side of this okay."

She made the tea and took the two cups into the living room. Tommy had eaten one of the sausage rolls and was now scoffing a doughnut—still in the beard and glasses. Did they make him feel anonymous, safe, even in her house? It was slightly unsettling to see him eating as though he didn't have a care in the world, when really, he should be shitting himself. Yes, she'd noted him displaying signs of being perturbed by what he'd done, but perhaps only because he might get caught. She'd seen a side to him she hadn't thought existed. If someone had come up to her and told her Tommy was a drug dealer, she'd have laughed in their face, but he *was* a drug dealer, and she'd benefited from that, albeit unknowingly, and now that she *did* know, she was doing her best to keep his antics hidden rather than doing the right thing by telling the police or even the twins.

Was that the wrong thing to do?

She sat on the armchair, placed her mug on a coaster, and took one of the sausage rolls out of the bag. She bit into it, watching her boy—and Ralph, on the other side of the room, watched her, or more specifically, watched for any flakes of pastry that might fall that he could come and scavenge.

A muscle twitched in Tommy's jaw. "I've been over it and over it, and I don't think I fucked up anywhere apart from using my van—which I'll need to bleach—taking your car to the woods, despite changing the number plate, and that sodding sleeping bag."

"Did you see anyone at the woods?"

"Yeah, some woman walking her dog, but she didn't look over at any of the other cars that were parked there, just got in hers and drove away."

That settled Cheryl somewhat, that her car may not have been clocked, but her Chimp switched to another topic. What if Leonora had been alive last night and she'd got up and walked to get help, then she'd collapsed somewhere else and had yet to be found? Or she had been found and the police were keeping it quiet. Or it was all over social media and they just didn't know it because they hadn't checked. The police could have already been watching Daffodil Woods, out of sight, and seen Tommy go there. They could have followed him, they could know he was at her place, that it was him who'd—

She cut her thoughts off before they went even more haywire, busying her mind by logging on to Facebook on her phone and scrolling one of the local pages—this was how to control her mind, by finding out facts instead of speculating on an unknown set of events in the future.

No one had mentioned a body being discovered, but someone had asked if they knew how long the French Café would be closed for. Someone else complained about the lack of parking outside Hair Trend Salon, and a lot of the other posts were asking if there were any houses to rent or employment to be had. She checked

BBC News, then the local online paper, and with no mention of a body, she relaxed. Or relaxed as much as she could in the circumstances.

"Nothing's been discovered as far as I can see online," she said, a tad breathless. "Maybe it'd be an idea to get rid of your van."

"I could park it round the back of the showroom and use one of the cars instead for now, but it's not going to stop the police asking anyone who's got the same van what they were doing that night regardless of whether the number plate matches or not."

"I know, I already thought of that, but out of sight, out of mind, if you catch my drift."

"Actually, it doesn't matter whether I hide the van or not, because they'll just go on the DVLA database and get a list of people who own one. I'll hide it anyway, so I don't get pulled over, but it doesn't mean I'm safe."

"I know." She glanced outside through the net curtains to where the van was parked. She really didn't need it to be associated with her address either. "Can you go and do it now or at least go and park it somewhere else round here? We don't want my neighbours clocking it, do we."

What with him doctoring the number plate and not looking the same as usual, she could make out she had a builder in if anyone happened to ask.

Adrenaline flushed through her again, sending her cold and jittery.

Why don't you just fuck off, Chimp?

You could end up in prison.

If a van isn't associated with the body, then there's nothing to worry about. Be quiet. Stop trying to frighten me.

She stood, upset that the voice in her head, the one she'd successfully banished years ago, had now found its way back in. To stop herself from giving Tommy a clip around the earhole, she took her cup into the kitchen and drank her tea in there, staring out into the back garden and praying Leanora's body would never be discovered or, if she was alive, she'd never recall any information that would help in putting the light of suspicion on Tommy.

Everything would be all right, wouldn't it?

Her Chimp laughed.

Chapter Twenty

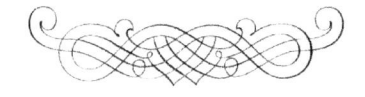

Sandra Deptford didn't mind being a grass if it meant she didn't have to slog her guts out. For too long she'd had several jobs to keep the household afloat, and to be able to stay at home, pretending she was on benefits, was a gift from the twins. She had to snitch on people, but whatever. Family came first. The thought of being able to clean her house from top to bottom was also a weight off her mind. She never seemed to have the time to keep her place in order, and small things had slipped by the wayside, like keeping the insides of the windows washed so mushy black mould didn't congregate in the corners of the sills.

Time enough for that, though. She was off to the corner shop to buy something nice for dinner, having taken the first envelope of wages in cash from George. It was going to take some time for her to come to terms with the fact she didn't have to pinch pennies anymore, and she thought she'd always hunt out a bargain no matter how much she had in her pocket, but she was definitely going to have a splurge. The Co-op had some buckets of fake KFC in the freezer, and she'd do microwave chips to go with it and buy some cakes for pudding. She'd get a couple of bottles of pop and maybe boxes of Pop Tarts as a big treat for breakfast in the morning. That didn't mean she was going to feed her children junk food from now on, but they'd been so good, never complaining about the meals she put on the table, and they deserved to be able to let loose every now and again.

She'd have to be careful regarding her story that she was now on benefits. Most of her neighbours were the nosy kind who'd notice if she started splashing out excessively. She'd bet the woman over the road had already clocked that the twins had visited her, but she'd been given the green light to tell anyone who asked that they'd been there to enquire about Sally's boss, Leanora—in fact, she'd been encouraged to talk about it just in case anyone had any pertinent information she could pass on to them.

The shop doors automatically parted, and she stepped inside, picking up a basket. She'd already taken a few quid out of the envelope and put it in her purse, and the woman who regularly worked behind the counter wouldn't think it odd that Sandra was actually using cash because she always did in here—she got cash tips from random people at the covered market. She walked the shop and collected everything she needed, adding a few share bags of sweets that they could eat later while watching Netflix, which she planned to get when she got home. The younger kids might ask questions regarding that, so she'd say Sally had been paid and had offered to sign up for the streaming service. The fact that

Sally's money was usually used to help buy food would likely be commented on, so maybe Sandra could say a big bonus had been involved.

Just these little things that needed to be squared away was a good indication of what her future would be like working for the twins. She was going to have a lot of spare money with no way to say where it had come from. Unless she said she'd found a job working from home. That could work.

She joined the queue behind a neighbour, Harriet, who spoke to some woman from the next street over who was annoyed about a van being parked half outside her house which had partially blocked her driveway. She hadn't been able to use her car to come to the shop, and when she'd knocked on the door of her neighbour, Cheryl, no one had answered.

"And she's in because I heard the telly."

"Who does the van belong to?" Harriet asked.

"Her son's got one, but this one's not the same number plate. It's bloody inconsiderate to have parked it there if you ask me."

It was on the tip of Sandra's tongue to butt in and make a comment that she was surprised this dilemma hadn't been put on the local Facebook page yet. It consisted of so many things like this, gripes that really didn't need to be aired on a public forum.

"Well, I've taken a picture of it," the woman said, "so I'm going to report it."

"That's a bit unnecessary," Harriet said. "Just pop a note through the letterbox and ask if the van can be moved along a tad."

It was the grumpy woman's turn to be served, and Harriet rolled her eyes at Sandra and whispered, "She was whinging about this *all the way* to the shop."

Sandra smiled. "Oh dear. Are you walking back with her as well?"

"Unfortunately."

Once Sandra had paid for her things, she thought nothing more of it, returning home to pop the shopping away and have a much-needed cup of tea. Then she tackled the cleaning of the kitchen with Sally's help until it was time to pick the smaller kids up from school.

She could get used to this life.

On the way back from St Swithin's Primary, Sandra happened to walk down the road where Harriet lived. There was no van to be seen, but there was an argument going on outside one of the houses. The grumpy woman was there, poking a finger towards someone. Sandra had to squint to make her out, but she reckoned it was Cheryl Coda. Mindful that an argument between women could result in a lot of swearing, hair-pulling, and scratching, Sandra ushered her children around the small crowd and told the kids to run until they reached the postbox a few metres ahead.

"First one there wins a bag of Haribo," she said.

They ran off, and Sandra caught the tail end of a sentence.

"… wasn't even a van there anyway, you're going mad."

"So you're saying I'm seeing things," Mrs Grumpy said, "when I damn well looked out of my window and saw the fucking thing there? I couldn't use my car because half my drive was blocked off. So I imagined that, did I? I imagined I had to walk to the shop instead with this cold wind freezing my tits off."

"You could do with the exercise," Cheryl sniped.

"You cheeky fucking cow, saying I'm fat! What's going on, then, for you to pretend there wasn't a van here? What are you up to?"

Sandra pressed on, catching up with the children and steering them around the corner towards her own street, and she got to thinking. Mrs Grumpy said there had been a van, Cheryl said there hadn't. *Was* she hiding anything? And if she was, shouldn't the twins be told about it?

Conscious she had to earn her money, she chivvied the children home, dished out bags of Haribo plus an extra one to the winner, then took out the little burner phone the twins had given her. Stomach rolling over, partly from excitement and partly from nerves, she typed in her first message.

SANDRA: THIS MIGHT NOT BE ANYTHING TO WORRY ABOUT, BUT CHERYL CODA HAD A VAN AT HER HOUSE EARLIER AND SHE'S DENYING IT EXISTS.

GG: PHONE YOU IN TWO SECS TO DISCUSS.

She closed the kitchen door, not wanting her kids to hear her side of the discussion. Her involvement with the twins was best kept a secret from everyone except Sally.

Chapter Twenty-One

He'd opted for a posh restaurant to show off, then wished he'd gone for something a bit more downmarket in case she expected to be wined and dined like this every time they went out. He was going to have to make it clear what was happening.

"I chose this place because it's a special occasion. I don't normally come here, see."

"It's beautiful. I can't imagine feeling comfortable enough to come here all the time. I'm grateful to you for bringing me here, it's just I'm used to my favourite café in Lille."

"Would you prefer to go somewhere else? We haven't ordered yet, so it won't be a problem, and I hate the thought of you feeling uncomfortable."

They ended up in a pub down the road, and she looked a lot more at home amongst the working and middle classes. They had pie, mash, and gravy, sticky toffee pudding and custard, and a nice creamy latte. After, he walked her towards his place along the Thames, and as the houses became gradually more upmarket, he sensed she became tense.

"Don't let the grandness of my gaff put you off," he said. "It's just bricks and mortar at the end of the day."

She nodded and linked her arm with his, the first contact she'd made since the hug she'd given him when she'd arrived. It was strange to know her so well yet not at all, and now he was in her company he was a little on edge. It was easier to write in a chat box and say what you had to say without eyes dissecting your expression. Here in front of her was a whole new ballgame, one he wasn't too good at playing. For the first time, he wished he'd had a proper relationship before her so he knew what to expect, but he'd been all about one-night stands, feeling he was too young to settle down.

She was older than him, too. He'd only discovered that tonight, and it had put him on the back foot, annoyed because it was something he should have asked her near the beginning. She was more experienced than him. She'd been with someone before, for four years, and they'd split up two years ago because he'd been controlling. Tommy would have to be careful how he manipulated her. He'd have to do it gradually so she didn't notice it happening.

They stopped outside his house, and she stared up at it, her eyes wide. It was impressive, even he could admit that. His kid self would have wet his pants at the thought of living here, yet now, as an adult, he took it for granted.

"Do you want to go in and have a look around on your own?" he asked. "I don't want to put any pressure on you by being right behind you, and it could also be a bit overwhelming."

She nodded and nipped past him when he opened the door, going inside to explore. He locked up and waited for her in the kitchen, wondering what her reaction would be to the fact he'd put her suitcases in a spare bedroom. He'd done it on purpose so it looked like he hadn't assumed she'd get into his bed. He planned to reel her right in. Make her believe he was a gentleman.

She returned downstairs. "I have a room of my own?"

"Only if that's what you want. I wasn't sure so… You're welcome in my room, of course you are, but I didn't think it was cool to presume. That's one thing we haven't talked about."

"But we did *talk about sex, and I thought you'd realise because of that, it meant I'd share your bed."*

"Unless you tell me outright, I'll never assume," he lied.

She smiled at that and came over to put her hands around his neck. She kissed him, and just for tonight he'd let himself fall into whatever pattern emerged, to feel what it was like to be in love with someone, and then tomorrow he'd put his guard back up. He had the stupid idea that one day she'd turn out just like him, a woman intent on making loads of money, his partner in crime and willing to help him sell the drugs. It might never happen, though, she had too much of a moral compass, but if he planted the right seeds, maybe he could nurture her bad side.

Everyone had one, didn't they?

Chapter Twenty-Two

George liked it when it seemed things were coming together. They'd spent the day asking questions regarding Leanora but hadn't discovered an awful lot that was of any use. Now Sandra had told them the snippet of information about a van outside Tommy's mum's gaff, his interest had been piqued and he wished he'd got their man, Moody, to follow Tommy's movements after they'd paid him that house visit.

As he hadn't listened to Sandra's little story on speakerphone, he related it to Greg who was driving them towards Tommy's house. They'd already been to his showroom, threatening the employees to keep their mouths shut that they'd been poking around. They'd also popped to the local leader's office (a booth in a pub) to let them know that they'd been asking questions on their patch and had been given permission to continue to do so should they need to. No one was allowed to kill Tommy in that area of South London except for the leader, though. The twins could do what they liked on their own Estate, and they wouldn't be so stupid as to murder him on someone else's turf.

"If nothing untoward was going on, why would she deny that a van had been outside her house?" Greg turned down Tommy's street.

"Exactly what Sandra was saying." George peered across when they passed Tommy's property. The van wasn't there either. "I'll get hold of that manager fella at the car showroom to let me know if that van turns up there as well as Tommy."

"Yeah, I wasn't that bothered about a van being parked outside his house when we paid him a visit because I didn't think it had anything to do with Tommy, because in my mind, the van she was placed in belonged to the man in the clown mask, but we've likely missed a trick here and they could be the same person, what with him having that supposed shaving cut on his face."

"We need to have another chat with Tommy."

George sent a message to the chap at the showroom, Lionel, who was now firmly in their pocket. A response came quickly that Tommy wasn't there but he'd dropped the van off, then cleaned the back out using bleach. George instructed Lionel to take the van to the East End and park it in a specific spot. He then arranged for Dwayne, their car thief, to collect it. He explained things to Greg, then got on with getting Moody to come and do surveillance in Tommy's street.

Pleased with himself for taking on Sandra, whose info could already have yielded good results, George said to Greg, "Never underestimate the casual eavesdropper, eh?"

"Sandra?"

"Yeah. She's ideal for the job. No one would think she'd pass that information on to us. I think we need to pay Cheryl Coda a visit, don't you?"

"If you say so, but if she's anything like our mum, you'll get nothing out of her. She'll stick up for her kid no matter what."

"I know, but there'll be expressions she can't hide or control, and they'll tell us everything we need to know."

Greg did a U-turn and headed towards Cheryl's. "We could also have a chat with the woman who had an arse on about the van being in the way."

"With any luck she might have written down the number plate if she's that nosy."

"We can but hope."

That reminded George about the number plate of the van owned by Clown Mask. The reg had come back as fake, which didn't surprise him.

Ten minutes later, Greg parked a fair way down the next street—the BMW might stick in someone's mind if they parked it in Cheryl's. George fished in the glove box for beards and glasses, then he handed over a beanie hat and stuck one on his own head. Next came puffa jackets. Disguises in place, they exited the car and walked down the road, George veering off up the garden path that belonged to Cheryl's neighbour. Greg remained by the gate, and George tapped on the door.

A sour-faced woman opened it, greying hair wispy at the sides, the rest in a lank ponytail. She folded her arms and tsked. "What do you want?"

George whispered, "Keep this under your hat, but it's George and Greg Wilkes. I don't have to tell you what will happen if you blab to anyone that we're here, do I?"

She eyed them. "No. So she went *that* far, did she? She actually told you I had the audacity to complain that whoever was at her house earlier blocked my driveway with their sodding van."

"She never told us, no, someone else did. What's your name?"

"Mrs McCready."

"Right. Far from us coming here to have a go at you, I'd like to know what you remember about this van and the person driving it."

"I took a picture of it, actually, because I was going to put it up on the Facebook group to shame the driver into coming out and moving it, but he buggered off before I could do it. Hang on." She dipped into a room to her left then returned holding a mobile up, the screen pointing towards George. "There you go."

He pulled his work phone out and took a picture of her photo. "Cheers. What did the driver look like?"

"I took a picture of him an' all." She swiped across and showed him the next image. "Now, when the van first came, it wasn't this fella who was driving it, it was Tommy, Cheryl's son. He went off in Cheryl's car with the dog, but the person who came back in the car with the dog was the man in that picture who then later took the van away."

George took a copy of the man's face; it wasn't difficult to see this bearded fucker was Tommy. "Thanks for your help, it's much appreciated." He withdrew an envelope from his pocket and handed it over. "Buy yourself something nice."

He left her and joined Greg at Cheryl's gate. Together they walked up her garden path, and Greg knocked on the door.

"She's not there," McCready said, still standing in her doorway. "She went out in her car not long after that bloke took the van. She had the dog with her. She went out earlier as well—she didn't have the dog then. What I dislike was when I confronted her about her allowing someone to be selfish enough to block my drive, she was telling me the van wasn't there at all when I knew damn well it was because I had a picture. If she's hiding the fact a van was there then you can almost guarantee something dodgy is going on."

George didn't miss living in a street where every single little thing became a big drama, but this particular drama had brought them to this point in time where in his eyes, something was going on with Tommy and Cheryl, and even if it didn't have anything to do with Leanora, he wanted to know what it was.

"Would you mind giving me a ring when she gets back?" he asked, taking a business card with just a phone number on it from his pocket.

"No need." She nodded down the street. "She's back now."

George imagined McCready was going to stay put for the time being, so when Cheryl got out of her car with a collie, he gave her one of his stares to let her know he'd prefer their conversation to go on behind closed doors. Cheryl got the gist and skirted around him and Greg on the path, sticking her key in the lock and letting the dog go in first. George and Greg followed her down the hallway into a kitchen where the dog lapped at a bowl of water and she pulled off a pair of yellow wellies.

"Where have you been?" George asked.

"Took the dog for a run."

"Where's Tommy?"

"No bloody idea. He was here earlier, but I haven't seen him since."

"The bloke with the beard, that was Tommy."

"No, it was a mate of his. Tommy came here to pick the dog up and go for a walk, but something came up to do with work so he got his mate to drop my car back. The mate stayed for a bit of lunch, then he left."

"Do you often let your son's mate stay in your house when you're not here?"

Cheryl chuffed out of breath. "Next door's been talking, has she? Nosy cow. Yes, he stayed here. I've known him years."

"What's his name?"

"None of your bloody business. He was fixing a leak under my bath." She pointed to the ceiling where a brown stain spoke of a leak at some point but quite some time ago, considering it wasn't damp.

"It hasn't leaked recently."

"Nope, I had had a washing-up bowl under the pipe and had to wait until I had enough money to pay for it to be fixed."

"Isn't that something a son would pay for on behalf of his mother if she was a bit strapped?"

"Yes, but I didn't want to bother him with it. Look, why are you even here?"

"The van that was here earlier. Is it Tommy's?"

"I don't know what van you're talking about."

"I think you do, but we'll leave it there." George stared at her. "For now."

They turned and walked out, striding down the street to the BMW. On the way here, George had sent a message to one of their surveillance men to come round and keep an eye on Cheryl's place. The fella currently sat in a dark-blue van across the street.

In the car, seat belts on, Greg drove off. Neither of them spoke for a while.

"We're being played," Greg said.

"Yep."

George took the phone out and checked any messages that had come in while they'd been talking to Cheryl. Dwayne had responded that Tommy's van was now at the warehouse. Moody had sent an update that Tommy had yet to return to his house. George sent a message to their private detective who had the means to test the back of the van for anything that would prove Leanora had been in it, regardless of Tommy cleaning it with bleach. George passed on the van's location.

"Shall we go and have another chat with Leanora?" he asked.

Greg nodded. "Do you reckon we should have taken Cheryl to the warehouse?"

"Maybe. We'll go back and pick her up later."

George stared out of the window for the rest of the journey. When Greg pulled up outside the safe house, George caught sight of Will standing at the window. They exchanged waves, then George and Greg entered the building. Leanora stood in front of the cooker, stirring something in a saucepan.

"That smells nice," George said.

The twins sat at the table with Will and explained what had been going on today.

"I'm inclined to think he had a beard and glasses on because he didn't want anyone to know what he was doing while he had his mum's dog," Will said.

"Yeah, you don't put a disguise on for no reason, do you?" George pinched his chin. "Are you *sure* you don't think he's capable of hurting you like the man in the clown mask?" he asked Leanora. "Because you said it felt like you'd been put in a van, and now all this shit about the van outside his mum's house and his mum saying it doesn't exist…it stinks of him confessing to her and her covering it up."

"And with the van being dropped off at the showroom and cleaned…" Greg sighed.

The work burner went off, and George had a look at the screen.

MOODY: HE'S ROLLED UP IN A MERCEDES AND GONE INTO HIS HOUSE.

George passed on that information. "Right, now we know where he is, we'll go back and speak to his mother. If she doesn't want to talk, we'll take her to the warehouse. She'll be more inclined to chat there."

"What is the warehouse?" Leanora asked.

"You don't want to know," Will said.

George led the way out to the car, suggesting to Greg that they switch to their little van, change outfits, and put on their long wigs and beards before they turned up at Cheryl's. With the ultra-nosy McCready next door, George didn't want her clocking that it was them who'd come back, plus, if they received a message from her that two men had arrived, then he knew she could be trusted to pass on any information to them in the future.

Vehicle swapped and disguises on, they returned to Cheryl's. She opened the door and jumped at the sight of them, and it was clear her mind worked a mile a minute trying to work out who they were.

"Best you get your shoes and coat on," George said in his normal voice, not one of his persona's. "We're giving you the courtesy of not collecting you as the twins, so do us the courtesy of coming nice and quietly."

"What for?" she asked.

"You know what for."

"If it's about that bloody van…"

"Amongst other things."

"What about my dog? How long am I going to be? I'll need to let him out for a wee by ten."

"We've got a few questions to ask you, so bring him with you, plus any food he'll need for the foreseeable."

"I'll need to get a bowl as well…"

"That's all right, I'll come in while you do it. Wouldn't want you running out the back, would we."

Her shoulders sagged as though the realisation had hit her that she wasn't going to be able to get away. She went into the kitchen, George following.

"Why can't you ask the questions here?" she said over her shoulder.

"Because if Tommy knows I've got his mother at an undisclosed location, he's more likely to tell us the truth, isn't he."

"My Tommy wouldn't have done anything wrong." She put a clean dog bowl, some cans of food, and a fork in a carrier bag along with a couple of rubber toys.

"Your Tommy may well have done plenty," George said, "but I think you're aware of that, aren't you, otherwise, why pretend there wasn't a van here earlier when there was?"

"But there wasn't!" She clutched the bag to her chest.

George held his phone up with the relevant photo on the screen.

She paled.

He glared at her. "Pack it in with the lies. Come on, let's get going."

Chapter Twenty-Three

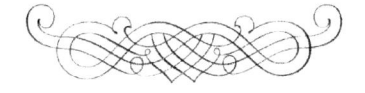

Cheryl shivered despite the big halogen heaters being switched on. They'd blindfolded her, and inside their destination, removed it to point her down some steps that had black rubber treads on them. This room was like a cellar with its glistening stone walls and what looked like spongy mould in the crevices. The faint rush of water came from somewhere, the Thames she'd spotted behind the building when she'd stared through the windscreen when they'd arrived. Ralph didn't seem to mind their surroundings, tippy-tapping along and having a good sniff, finding a trapdoor in the floor particularly interesting. Two chains hung from hooks in the ceiling above it, manacles on the ends. She didn't have to be that brainy to work out what they were for and could only hope she hadn't been brought down here in order to be strung up.

But that was going to be the inevitable outcome, because there was no way she was going to grass on her son in order to save herself. She'd rather die than betray him. She dismissed the small reminder in the back of her mind that she'd contemplated phoning the police earlier.

If we stick to our stories, everything will be okay.

Providing Tommy had told her the full truth. But what if he'd left a few things out? What if there was evidence, other than in the back of the van, the sleeping bag, and that lock-up that could be pinned on him? If only they knew where Leanora had gone they'd have been better placed to make plans, but as it was, Cheryl had been convincing herself that the woman had gone back to France. What if she hadn't? What if that was just a ruse to trick Cheryl and Tommy into thinking they were safe? Were the twins playing some kind of sick game?

George ran his hand down one of the chains, letting it go with a little push so it bashed into its companion and rattled. "Normally we put people straight on the chains, usually naked, because we find if we start as we mean to go on, the person we're interrogating tends to get the gist pretty fucking quickly. But I won't insult your intelligence. You seem like a clever woman. Basically, what we want to know is that if Tommy's had anything to do with Leanora from the French Café going missing, then we need to know about it."

"I was in town earlier. The café was shut, and someone said she'd gone to France. Why would you even think my Tommy would know anything about it?"

"Because they were a couple once upon a time and she lived with him."

"I wasn't aware of that."

"So you're not close to your son then?"

Cheryl didn't hide the flinch quickly enough, and she knew George had caught it by the smirk that pulled at his mouth. Fuck it, she didn't like anyone to know there was a flaw in their relationship, where Tommy was secretive—more secretive than she'd ever imagined.

"Close enough," she said, "but he has his space to do his own thing. It would be weird if he told me everything, don't you think?"

That was the only concession she'd make in letting George know she hadn't been in the know about all of Tommy's life. He'd insisted that if he got caught then she was to claim innocence regarding the drugs and the murder—and she could have done that successfully had he not confessed to her, but it was done now, there was no changing it, and she'd have to do what he'd suggested and act shocked if the twins presented her with any findings. It would still feel like a betrayal, even though they'd agreed she'd do that, but Tommy had been insistent that she didn't take any blame. If he found out she'd pretended the van hadn't been outside her house, he'd probably tell her off for it. In hindsight she'd been stupid, far too eager to paper over the cracks of truth, and in a world that was full of smartphones and video doorbells, she now realised she'd been so bloody thick.

"Fine, there *was* a van," she said, "but I told my neighbour there wasn't because I wanted to shut her up, make her look stupid. I didn't realise it'd been parked halfway across her precious driveway, which she shouldn't even have because it's supposed to be a front garden."

"She can turn it into a place to park her car if she wants."

Cheryl shrugged. "Anyway, that's why I lied, to piss her off. The van is Tommy's."

"Why does he drive round in that rather than a car from his showroom?"

"It was his dad's. Probably sentimental, I don't know."

"Are you divorced from his old man?"

"We never got married. He didn't want anything to do with me once he left us, and he's dead now, so good riddance. He gave the van to Tommy in his will—finally acknowledging he had a son when it was too late."

"The man with the beard at your house…"

"Tommy's friend."

"Come on, you know damn well it's Tommy with a beard and glasses. I've seen a fucking picture, it's obvious."

She tried to recall what Tommy had told her to say if any questions like this came along. "Okay, yes, it was him. He came to mine to collect the dog and take my car up to Daffodil Woods."

George raised his eyebrows. Shit, why had he done that at the mention of the woods?

"Someone owes him some money for a car," she babbled to get his mind off whatever had bothered him, "and Tommy knew where he'd be, so he followed him, but he couldn't find him along any of the trails so he brought my dog back to mine."

"Why was he in a disguise?"

She raised her arms and let them slap down on her sides. "Think about it. Bloke owes him a lot of money. Bloke sees Tommy coming and legs it. If Tommy had a beard on, he was less likely to have been recognised, then he could have got right up to him and explained who he was and that they needed a chat." She gestured to George. "You two have got beards and wigs on to stop my neighbours knowing you were round my house, it's no different. People use disguises all the time."

"True. Why not just tell us this in the first place?"

"Because I didn't know whether he'd be in trouble for intimidating a customer. I didn't know whether Daffodil Woods is classed as being on your Estate."

"Fair enough. Is that your final story?"

She nodded. "It's the only one I've got," she lied.

Chapter Twenty-Four

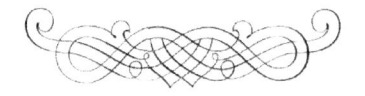

The cracks had splintered the veneer of Tommy's life all too quickly. He hadn't expected it to happen so fast, her cottoning on to what he was up to. He'd asked where she was, expecting her to give him a blow-by-blow account of her day. How stupid he'd been to do that when she'd left her former partner because of his controlling nature, so of course *she was*

looking out for it now. Tommy had failed at being clever enough to fool her, and she'd just told him it wasn't working out so she was going to move into the café flat.

"What?"

Across the island in the kitchen, she said, "I told you about my ex and how he made me feel. You know how vulnerable I was when I was with him and yet you've chosen to do the same thing. We can exist together without you knowing exactly what I'm doing, you just can't seem to accept that I am allowed to have my own life as well as being with you. I won't put up with it, and you won't stop being manipulative, so I'm leaving. It's for the best. I've already packed my cases. I knew from last night's behaviour that it was time for me to go."

Part of him was gutted. He enjoyed having sex on tap and someone to cook dinner with him. He'd planned for her to cook it alone in the future, but it seemed there would be no more weeks rolling by in order for him to effect the change. It was so strange because they'd had a whirlwind romance and they'd fallen for each other so quickly, yet she'd fallen out of love just as fast. He'd become cocky, complacent, convinced she'd never leave, and her announcement that she was walking out on him had brought him down several pegs.

How had it come to this? He should never have assumed he could dominate this relationship. She may have given him the impression she was willing to take direction, but she still had too much of a backbone for him to be able to control her.

How had he believed she'd be malleable?

He watched her walk out of the room. Didn't even bother to chase her up the stairs and plead with her to stay. Maybe deep down he didn't want her to. Maybe his subconscious knew that her living with him wasn't a good thing and vice versa. He was confused by his feelings, how anger floated through him one minute because she'd had the brass neck to stand up for herself, then bewilderment that she even wanted to leave after saying she loved him. His father had done that, said he cared and then fucked off. Maybe that was why Tommy never wanted to have a relationship. Maybe that was why he kept his distance from his mother, only going to see her every now and again, because if you cared, then you got hurt.

He listened to the creak of the floorboards above, then the bump and clatter of her bringing the suitcases downstairs. If he was the gentleman he'd tried to fool her into believing he was, then he'd have gone out there to help her carry them despite her leaving him, but she'd not long told him he was turning into a manipulating monster and that she didn't want him anywhere near her, so she could deal with it on her own.

"Don't touch me," was what she'd said when he'd reached for her. "Keep your bloody hands away from me."

She wheeled two suitcases down the hallway, didn't even pause at the front door. She swung it open and hefted the cases outside, pushing them to the back of a cab that idled at the kerb. The driver got out to place them in the boot, and she climbed into the back, facing straight ahead. She'd left the front door open in her haste to get away from him, so he strolled down the hallway and stood there while the taxi drove off. Not once did she glance to her right to look at him.

He should have known this would be the outcome. Back when they'd been talking online, he'd sensed he was more into her than she was into him, but as usual, he'd thought he knew best and could navigate the situation to his advantage. He'd believed he could mould her, when in fact, she was rigid when it came to being manipulated. No matter the beautiful house, no matter the meals out and the flowers and the presents, none of it meant a thing to her when her well-being was compromised.

He kind of had to admire her for that.

He closed the front door, unable to tell her he was sorry, which he was, but he'd never admit it. He'd got used to her being around, her laughter, the stories she'd tell about the customers in the café. He'd allowed himself to feel too much, and it was his own stupid fault that this had gone so fucking wrong.

He sent a message to the Unidenticals.

TOMMY: ARE YOU STILL UP FOR THE NEW GIG AT THE CAFÉ?

NOJO: YEP. WILL SEND OUR UPDATED PRICE LIST OVER.

A screenshot came through, and Tommy studied the numbers.

Leanora may have walked out on him, but a woman who wasn't in it for the long haul wasn't someone he wanted to be with anyway. He imagined the Unidenticals scaring the shit out of her and decided that she *ought to get up in the night to let them into the storeroom. He'd originally planned for them to use a key and do the deals while she slept, but if he could unsettle her life by making her become a part of the drug sales, then he'd have something over her.*

He'd have control, even if she never realised it.

Chapter Twenty-Five

The Unidenticals stood in the darkness down the side of the Noodle. The pub was in the middle of a housing estate, so plenty of properties around, lots of potential witnesses for later. Not that Noel cared, because they had their trusty balaclavas on. Their mate inside the pub had let them know their target had arrived, so they'd driven to the next street over, left their nicked car outside a house with a red front door, and walked to the pub. They'd received a couple of looks from a bloke and his missus on the other side of the road, and Noel had marvelled at how frightened they were by a face mask. He supposed they *did* appear scary, but he was so used to seeing his brother with one on that it failed to make an impact.

"Send a message so our man can get the target to come outside," Joel said.

Using a throwaway burner, Noel did that and waited for a response. A thumbs-up emoji appeared, so he switched the phone off and shoved it in his jacket pocket, doing up the zip so it didn't fall out while they were scrapping. Coming out from the side of the pub, they stood with their backs against a six-foot wooden fence that separated the tarmac at the front of the boozer from a resident's property next door. It was dark enough that they were shrouded in shadows, but the lights along the top of the Noodle door gave off enough illumination that when their mate and the target came out, they were easily seen.

"Fuck it," their mate said, "I need to nip back in and have a piss."

The target lit a cigarette, pacing in a circle. Noel waited until two more puffs had been inhaled, then he nudged his brother in the ribs. They stepped forward as one unit, the bloke they were after clocking them in his peripheral and spinning to face them.

"'Ere, hold up! What's going on?"

Noel studied him. Squat body. Black hair. Wonky nose, like he'd been in several bust-ups before. Ugly as fuck.

"We've been asked to send you a message," Noel said.

"Who from?"

"You should have some idea of who you might have pissed off."

"I haven't upset anyone."

Noel snorted. "Bollocks."

"Who are you?"

"Think 'seeing double'."

The bloke paled. "The Brothers?"

Noel had given out false information, like they usually did regarding the twins in these situations, so when they left the scene, nothing would be done about the upcoming beating. No police, nothing.

Noel and Joel lashed out, the bloke going down to his knees fairly quickly. He lurched backwards from a scathing uppercut, landing on his side, his cheek whacking on the tarmac. Joel put the boot in, avoiding the man's skull—cracked and broken ribs were enough of a warning for now. One wrong kick in the head could spell an unwanted fatality, and unless that was what they were paid to do, then they weren't going to risk it.

"Oi, what's your game?" someone shouted. They'd stopped their vehicle coming out of the car park at the back, the passenger having wound the window down to call out to them.

Noel nudged Joel again, and they strutted off down the street as though they didn't have a care in the world. They kept their balaclavas on even when they were in the car driving away. So long as the victim realised the beating had been a warning and he did as he was told going forward, everything was going to be hunky-dory.

If he didn't…then the Unidenticals would be back.

Chapter Twenty-Six

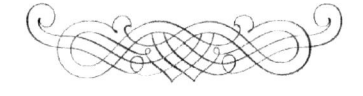

Tommy had read messages from the two customers who were going to buy the rest of the drugs—all was sorted there. He'd let the Unidenticals know what time they'd be arriving and where, plus that he'd let the man he bought drugs from know that he wasn't continuing that side of his business any longer. He'd do what

Mum said and jack the drugs in. But he didn't want to think about that. He had something more pressing on his mind at the minute.

He'd been ringing Mum for the past couple of hours and, with no response, which was unlike her, he'd made the decision to go round there. On the way, he was sure he'd been followed by someone in an older-model brown car, although whoever it was had hung back once Tommy had turned onto her housing estate. He'd shrugged it off as paranoia—he'd suffered with that a lot recently. He'd driven past the Noodle and seen the Unidenticals in their balaclavas beating the shit out of someone, but he'd kept going. Sod getting involved there, especially if they were pulling their usual stunt in pretending to be The Brothers.

The least Tommy had to do with any of them the better.

There had been times in his life when he had the sudden urge to pack a bag and fuck off. Tonight was one of them. Life had got a little too overwhelming for his liking, and for someone who usually had all his ducks in a row, his conscience clear, and felt content that his world spun right, it was unnerving to feel the complete opposite.

The only thing he felt in control of was this vehicle.

The only contentment he had was…fuck, there wasn't any.

"Fucking wonderful. It's all going to shit."

Tommy turned up at his mother's with a massive sense of unease in his gut—nothing new, he'd been anxious for a while now—and he didn't know what to do with the emotions, the sensations: tight chest, a near constantly rolling-over tummy, and that weird cold that chilled his legs and sent them to jelly.

He glanced out of the window. "Oh, for fuck's sake…"

Mrs McCready from next door. Just what he needed. She came out onto her path as he exited the car, and he braced himself for trouble. Mum had messaged him earlier about the row they'd had. McCready was probably going to start on him now.

"Have you seen my mum?" he asked to head her off before she had a chance to get started.

"Oh, I've seen her all right. For some reason she thought it was a good idea to lie to me—or gaslight me, whichever way you want to look at it. Well, she'll soon see that was a mistake."

"What do you mean, she lied to you?"

"A van that was out here earlier—*blocking my drive*. You know damn well it was here because you were driving it, I saw you."

"What has she said then?"

"That the van wasn't even here. It doesn't exist. But I took pictures of it, didn't I, and her over the road's got one of them fancy doorbells, and she's going to take some screenshots for me."

Tommy was going to have to keep McCready onside if she was going as far as taking pictures. "I don't get why Mum's lying about the van. Of *course* it was here."

The woman smiled and seemed glad Tommy had agreed with her. "Yeah, then a man with a beard drove off in it later on."

"Do you think my mum's okay? Like, could she have had a mental breakdown or something? To say the van wasn't there when it was… It doesn't sound right, does it? A stroke? Dementia?"

McCready rubbed a finger over her bottom lip. "I didn't think of that, I just thought she was being a lying bitch."

"So have you seen her since?"

"Yes. She went off with two long-haired men in a van. Not the same van as yours, one of those smaller ones."

Long-haired men? Who the fuck were *they*?

"What time was that?" he asked, his sense of doom and gloom increasing.

"I can't rightly remember." McCready smirked as though she knew damn well when it was but she wasn't prepared to say.

Stomach lurching, Tommy got in the Mercedes and rang Mum again. The ringing stopped after a couple of goes, then silence, followed by breathing.

"Mum? Mum, are you okay?"

"She's fine," George said.

George. Fuck.

Tommy composed himself. "Um, why are you answering her phone?"

"Because it was in my pocket and I didn't want her to answer it. What do you want?"

"She hasn't been picking up my calls, and I need to know if she's all right."

"She is."

"Can I speak to her?"

A muffled sound, then: "Let your son know you're still breathing."

"I told them you went to the woods in a beard to see that customer," Mum said. "They're asking about the woman from the French Café, saying you were her boyfriend, but I didn't know anything about that. Why didn't you tell me you were seeing someone? They've said she's gone back to France. Did she tell you she was going?"

Okay, so she was sticking to their plan, saying what they'd agreed. Good.

"She walked out on me and hasn't spoken since," he said. "Are you okay?"

"I'm fine."

"That's enough now," George said. "Where are you, Tommy?"

"Sitting in my car outside Mum's. Why?"

George gave him directions. "Go there and wait."

The line went dead. Tommy caught sight of Mrs McCready at her front door, and it got right on his nerves that she had the balls to think it was okay to stand there so obviously watching him.

Unless the twins have asked her to keep an eye out…

That was more than likely, so he couldn't really blame her for doing as she was told. Still, he shook his head at her to show his displeasure and drove away, his mind shifting to something more important: why on earth he'd been told to go and park outside Our Lady of Saint Patrick's.

The twins had obviously collected Mum in disguise—they were the long-haired men. They'd asked her questions about Leanora. It meant if they'd picked Mum up, they felt Tommy had something to do with Leanora going missing. Yet Mum had mentioned the France thing again, so what was going on? Was Leanora missing or not? He was going to have to ask questions. Make them think he was pissed off at their assumption he'd had anything to do with her disappearance.

Unless they'd discovered more than Mum knew. Now Tommy came to think about it, they weren't the type to reveal all their cards at once. For all he knew, they could think she was hiding stuff, or they'd picked her up to ensure Tommy did as he was told and met them outside the church.

She was being used as a bargaining chip, a way to make him talk. He contemplated how he could spin it, if he admitted to murder, that killing

Leanora was justified. He could say she'd told him about selling drugs from the back of the café for some bloke or other. He'd got up in arms about it, saying it was wrong, and they'd argued, the row getting out of hand. He hadn't meant to hurt her, but he had, and he regretted it more than anything. He'd panicked and dumped her in the woods.

Would that fly with the twins? Would they believe he'd got arsey on their behalf? Unlikely. They'd want to know why he hadn't told him about this when they'd come to his house. The answer to that was easy enough. He'd committed murder and worried they'd punish him for it.

Kill him.

He parked outside the church and sat there for a moment, looking ahead then in the rearview mirror to see if anyone was coming. Then he checked to his right, staring at the church doorway. A priest stood there and beckoned for him to go inside.

Even the twins wouldn't be so crass as to lure him into a church and beat him up somewhere so sacred, would they?

I wouldn't put anything past them.

He got out of the car, blipped the lock, and walked towards the church, scouring the surroundings. Grass, trees, and over his shoulder, a park with several people walking their dogs. That made him feel marginally safer, but should he follow the priest into the building? Would he ever come out if he did? Once again, the not knowing did his head in, as did the indecision where he stood on the top step. He hadn't brought a weapon with him—hadn't even thought to, which was stupid, considering who'd told him to come here.

But is Mum inside? Is this where they took her?

He ended up following the bloke. The door wasn't ominously locked behind him, and the priest continued on ahead down the aisle, so unless someone was hiding on the floor between the pews, Tommy didn't expect anyone to jump up and lock him in.

But they could be waiting outside and will come in any minute.

He looked over his shoulder again, but no one was there.

"Let's go into the vestry where it's warmer," the priest said. "I'm Father Michael Donovan by the way."

Tommy entered the room. A standalone fire with fake flames blasted out heat where it stood randomly beside a filing cabinet, looking completely out of place without a surround or mantelpiece.

"Take a seat."

Tommy sat where Donovan pointed, an armchair with tartan cushions. Donovan sat behind the desk and poured tea from a pot into two mugs. He pushed one of them across the desk along with sweeteners in one of those clicky plastic packages and a pint carton of full-fat milk. Tommy supposed he could trust a priest not to poison him so accepted the drink with a nod.

"You're probably wondering what you're doing here," Donovan said.

"I was told to come by George."

"He wanted me to have a little chat with you, see if you're willing to answer honestly—if you do, then it means you won't have to go elsewhere."

"Elsewhere?"

"Um, they have a place. Where they… They're with your mother there."

Tommy frowned at him, a bit disgusted if he were honest. "I didn't realise your sort were happy to intimidate people for the twins."

"Oh, I'm not going to intimidate you, and I'm most certainly not happy to be doing…this…"

"What truth do they want me to tell?"

"Regarding the whereabouts of Leanora from the French Café."

"They seem to think she's gone to France, so they already know where she is."

"That's what certain people were told, and they let the twins know that. George and Greg know why that story was spun, to hide what's really been going on."

"Which is?"

"Someone tried to kill Leanora, but it didn't work. She's alive."

"Kill her?" Tommy had sounded sufficiently shocked, and he hoped he looked it, but on the inside, Jesus, they knew what had gone on. Had Mum blabbed? Or was it 'certain people'? Shit, was it the Unidenticals? Was that why Noel had said they wanted to keep their distance now?

Donovan nodded. "Yes, kill her, but you already know that, don't you?"

"Why the fuck would *I* know that?"

The priest appeared truly confused—as though he believed Tommy and it went against the fact he should always believe the twins. "Perhaps I've been misinformed. Perhaps your mother saying that you had killed Leanora and put her body inside a sleeping bag in the woods... They may well have misinterpreted that. That's what you're saying, isn't it, that they've got their facts wrong?"

Shit. So Mum's had to open her mouth. They must have put pressure on her. Hurt her. "Why would my mum even say that when it's lies?"

Donovan seemed to struggle with his conscience. "Dear God, this is so difficult. I'm going to be honest with you. I was told to say your mother had confessed what she knew, to get you to slip up. I'd really rather not be having this chat, it puts me in a horrible position—a man of God indulging in trickery and deception."

"Why do it then?"

"Because the twins are very helpful to the church. We have a new roof. We have new Bibles. We have new heating."

"So you owe them. You're under their thumb."

"I'm very grateful to them, and I can see how it would look like I'm being dishonest by associating with them, but I assure you, they are genuine men who like to help the community, and I'm a genuine man who'll take whatever's on offer if it means my parishioners benefit from it."

"Even if it means knowing they've got my mum somewhere and they've probably been nasty to her? I mean, that's how they work, isn't it? They threaten people. Get them to do what they want. I suspect they threatened *you*. They'd have said something that made you realise you have to do what they want, whether you like it or not. And you're just dressing it up as passing messages along to people like me. D'you know what? Fuck this. You do you and whatever makes you feel good about yourself."

"There's a lot to be said for confessing. You never know, if you tell the truth, they might not respond in the way you think."

"Listen, I don't know what the fuck's going on. I used be with Leanora. She moved out, we split up. The twins came round and asked me if I knew where she was. I said no. They told me she'd moved to France, and in my head, I'm thinking: *If you know she's gone to France, why are you asking me where she is?* Next thing I know, they've picked up my mum, and now I'm here."

"Do you like clowns?"

Tommy lifted the cup to his mouth and took a sip of tea. Then another. Christ, he hoped Donovan couldn't see his hand shaking. It couldn't be a coincidence that he'd mentioned clowns. "I don't feel one way or another about them. Why?"

"Because somebody in a clown mask collected some drugs from the café. The boxes the drugs were in were too heavy for the clown to lift, so they were removed from the box and placed in the back of a vehicle. The clown drove off, leaving the empty boxes behind. Leanora put the boxes in her storeroom."

Shit, shit, shit! So they must have spoken to her to know that. Or someone else was in the café when I went to get the drugs and they were watching me out of the window.

Tommy sighed. "Right…and that has something to do with me because…?"

"The fingerprints will be checked against yours. One of the reasons you're here is to keep you out of the way because there's a man in your house now, lifting prints for comparison. Are they going to match the ones on the boxes or even on that cup you're drinking from? The clown didn't wear gloves so…"

Tommy was going to be caught bang to rights, and there was fuck all he could do about it. He placed the cup on the desk. "Not saying I've done anything, but if I 'confess' to you, what happens then?"

"Someone will take you away for you to be spoken to further."

"Earlier, you said if I was honest that wouldn't happen. Or was that a lie an' all? Anyway, you'd have to let them know to come here and get me first. I could leave before they even have a chance to sit in their motor."

"Not when the person sent to collect you is standing out in the hallway right this second."

Tommy glanced at the doorway. No shadow on the wall to indicate someone stood there. *Is he fucking me about?* "What happens after I'm taken away?"

"You speak to the twins, and they'll decide what to do with you."

"And you're okay with that, are you? Your Christian self can sleep at night knowing that I might get killed?"

"I'll square my part in this with God."

"So you're saying He'll forgive you, will He, just because you'll say sorry? Does the same happen for me? I doubt it, so I'll keep my mouth shut, thank you very much, until there's proof I've done something."

He rose and walked across the vestry, poking his head out into the hallway. No one was there. So the priest was well into lying, was he, making shit up? Then a flicker of movement caught Tommy's eye, and someone stepped out of another doorway, a big bloke in a tartan suit. What the hell was it with the check pattern around here?

"I'm Jimmy," the bloke said. "I think it's probably best you come with me, don't you?" He smiled. "If you want your mother to remain free of bruises, that is."

The way he'd said it shit Tommy up, and the look on Jimmy's face told him he was better off doing as he was told. "My car's parked out the front."

"That's fine. Leave your keys with the father. He'll arrange for it to be moved."

Tommy turned to face the vestry and the priest who looked at him apologetically. While Tommy believed the Godly bloke experienced remorse, he didn't believe he felt too bad about Tommy being carted away, especially if he was under the impression he was a killer. He was probably thinking Tommy had a right cheek to peer down his nose at him for colluding with the twins when what Tommy had done was infinitely worse.

He passed the keys over. Jimmy placed his hand at the top of Tommy's back and guided him through the church and out the front. A nondescript black car stood parked behind the Mercedes, and someone sat in the back. The rear door opened, and Jimmy gave Tommy a nudge towards it.

"I don't think I need to cuff you, do I?" Jimmy said. "And anyway, Sonny's got a gun, so if you even think of fucking about, he'll shoot you."

Tommy's legs went cold and wobbly again. He got in the car, putting on his seat belt and acting as though he wasn't scared. He glanced at Sonny who held a gun in his lap pointed towards Tommy. Jimmy got in the driver's seat and set off.

"Where will my car be taken?" Tommy asked.

"That's the least of your worries," Sonny said. "Fucking hell, if I were you and I was being taken to see the twins, I'd be more worried about whether I was going to come out of it alive."

"But I haven't done anything wrong."

"Loads of people say that," Sonny said. "It never fails to amaze me how everyone tries to get out of it by lying, and there's no point, because in the end, the twins always get to the truth. My advice? Admit whatever you've done. It'll save so much pain in the long run."

Tommy doubted it. Considering George had such a bad temper, the second Tommy said he'd killed Leanora, he wouldn't be given a chance to explain why. But he *had* to remain hopeful that he'd get out of this somehow.

Sonny's words properly registered.

It'll save so much pain in the long run.

Pain. He meant torture, didn't he.

Fuck.

Chapter Twenty-Seven

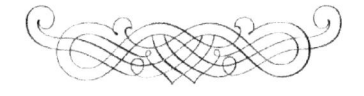

Father Michael had hated talking to Tommy the way he had, but although the twins hadn't threatened him to comply exactly, it was obvious he had to do as he was told or face the consequences. It didn't matter to them that he was a man of God. All right, maybe they'd be a little bit lenient towards him, giving him more second chances than anyone else if ever he messed up, but he had a feeling he was only fooling himself there. If he pissed them off he'd be tortured until he was truly sorry or they'd killed him. He didn't want to face either scenario, hence why he did as they said. He was well aware what he'd said about doing this for the parishioners was lame, an excuse for appalling behaviour that would be frowned upon if someone else did it.

He stood at the church door and watched the black car drive away, wondering if Tommy's life would cease to exist within the hour. From what he'd been told, the man had murdered a French woman, who'd somehow come back to life, telling a tale about drugs and two men in balaclavas and one in a clown mask. It all sounded like a film to be honest, but Michael had learned from other stories the twins had told him that real life was sometimes weirder than fiction.

He sighed and locked the door, walking down the aisle and entering the vestry. He stood in front of the fire with his phone in hand, contemplating whether to send The Brothers a message or if he should ring them instead. The problem with ringing them was that he risked hearing

Tommy's mother being hurt in the background, and he didn't think he could stomach it.

He took the coward's way out and sent a text.

MICHAEL: JIMMY AND SONNY HAVE THE PACKAGE.

The reply came swiftly.

GG: SO YOU COULDN'T GET HIM TO TALK THEN?

MICHAEL: HE'S ACTING LIKE HE HASN'T DONE ANYTHING.

GG: I TOLD JIMMY TO LEAVE AN ENVELOPE IN THE STOREROOM FOR YOU.

MICHAEL: THANK YOU.

At the beginning of this strange relationship with the twins, Michael had told himself that if he put any money he received into the church then his actions in whatever they asked him to do were justified. Sometimes, though, he took a few notes out for himself, then had to go to one of the other churches to confess his sin. It had become a nasty little habit, taking more and more each time, and it was something he needed to stop doing.

He'd become a criminal.

He left the vestry and nipped across the hallway into the storeroom. Every time he came in here he remembered the Christmas fayre and the televisions that had been stored here then subsequently stolen. He looked around at the cardboard boxes containing teabags, coffee, and sugar, packets of biscuits for any meetings at the church, and numerous other items the twins had donated. It was like Tommy had said, Michael was in their pocket and there was nothing he could do about it—and if he walked away, they'd find him, so what was the point?

He spied the envelope on one of the shelving units screwed into the wall. Taking it down, he opened it and inspected the contents. By the thickness of the wad, he'd been given more than usual, and they were twenty-pound notes, too, not tenners. It wouldn't hurt just this once to split the money in half, would it? The twins had near enough paid for everything that needed doing in the church, and every week the biscuits and things were delivered, not to mention the sandwiches from the bakery when the book club came for their afternoon session on a Wednesday. He couldn't think what the church's half of the money would be used for, so maybe he could keep all of it this time?

He imagined George smiling. The man had told him from the start that the money was for Michael to keep. Michael had insisted he wouldn't touch a penny, and George had said that eventually, he would.

It didn't sit well that George had been right.

If Michael had a propensity for swearing, he would, but he didn't, so he stuffed all the money in his pocket. He switched the fire off in the vestry, locked up, and left the church via the back, making his way to the Catholic St Mary's.

He had a confession to make.

Chapter Twenty-Eight

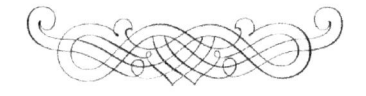

Cheryl had tried not to cry, but it was difficult when her son was being brought here so George could force the truth out of him—the proper truth. He said she had to stand and watch, that was her punishment for her part in this mess—he reckoned for a mother that was enough torture. What he hadn't said was how he'd kill her afterwards. She prayed for a quick bullet to the forehead.

Even though she hadn't wanted to come here and cave in, she'd confessed. She hadn't thought the twins would believe her, that she hadn't known anything until her son had so recently spilled the beans, but George had looked at her with pity.

She'd brought Tommy up to be a good person, but somewhere along the line it had gone wrong. There had been a miscommunication in what she was trying to teach him—his need to make as much money as possible to keep the wolf from the door was, in her opinion, overblown and unnecessary. He earned enough money at the car showroom to live comfortably, so in her book he was being greedy.

She stood on top of the closed trapdoor, Ralph sitting beside her, his warm body leaning on her leg. George had poured water into a bowl, and he'd also fed the dog, then Greg had taken him out for a walk, coming back to say he might have to get a dog of his own he'd enjoyed it that much.

Would they look after Ralph after she and Tommy were killed? She couldn't imagine them taking a collie around the estate with them. She'd have thought they'd want a rottweiler or something, not her fluff ball. Tears stung her eyes at the thought of Ralph wondering where she was once she was dead, but then she remembered her punishment was watching her son die, so did that mean they were going to let her live? How could they when she could so easily open her mouth and tell people what they'd done? The police had been trying to bring the twins down for years. One word from her and…

"Will you just break my boy's legs and leave it at that?" she asked.

Then she went on to explain Tommy's reasoning, why he'd sold drugs, and she got the idea that George understood that all too well.

"When you grow up skint," he said, "and like us you watch your mother struggle, I get it, you just want to make your lives better, and that would have been okay for Tommy to do that had he let us know what he was up to. He's been selling drugs on our Estate, and that means he owes a fuck-ton of protection money. I doubt very much I'm going to get that back, unless he tells us where the drugs are stored and we can sell it to clear his debt, and ordinarily, if that was the only thing he'd done I'd probably just break his legs, fuck him up a bit, snap his fingers, maybe stick a corkscrew in his eye, but he tried to kill someone, an innocent woman who didn't deserve it, and he left her in the woods thinking she was dead. If that old boy hadn't found her and Tommy had got there first when he supposedly went after that client of his, then I doubt very much Leanora would be alive now. Your son's a fucking cunt, and he needs to be made aware of that."

Cheryl had always thought she'd fight right to the last knockings, but she could see by George's face it was a waste of time. He was set on what he planned to do, and she had no choice but to stand there and watch it happen.

"Will you kill me afterwards?" she asked, "because I don't think I can live with the images you're going to put in my head."

"If you want to die then you can fucking kill yourself. You brought that little scrote up so you can live with the consequences of his actions."

Cheryl got brave—after all, the worst thing she could ever imagine was going to happen when Tommy arrived, so what did it matter if George shouted at her for what she had to say? "Would you feel the same if it was *your* mother? *She* brought *you two* up. You say my Tommy's a cunt, but take a look at yourselves."

"I wouldn't badmouth my mum if I were you," Greg said.

She turned to stare at him. "Hit a nerve, did I?"

"Why don't you shut your fucking gob and go and stand over there before I do you some serious damage."

She smiled at him and clicked her fingers for Ralph to follow her to where Greg pointed. She sat on the cold floor in the corner, trying not to think about what lay ahead. Tommy was going to know she'd grassed him up, and she probably wouldn't be given the chance to tell him she'd tried her best to make it all better, but he'd know, wouldn't he? He'd understand why she'd had to speak up—he'd told her she had to if it came to it.

A monitor on the wall at the bottom of the stairs flickered to black-and-white life, and Cheryl made out three figures, one of the shapes the same as Tommy.

"Ah, here he is." George went off upstairs.

Cheryl watched the monitor to see what was going on up there. The warehouse door opened, George appearing, then the three guests went inside. She closed her eyes, tears falling, Ralph propping his chin on her knee.

The worst time of her life was about to begin.

Chapter Twenty-Nine

Tommy glanced around the warehouse. Halfway up the walls, a metal balcony. Cardboard boxes leaned against one another up there, and he assumed they contained either drugs or goods for resale. He'd had a thought on the way here, to offer the twins the remaining bricks of cocaine in exchange for his life. Then he'd leave London and never come back. The problem was, it would mean telling them where the drugs were, and that would drop the Unidenticals in the shit—if Mum hadn't done that already. But then if Tommy was legging it, it didn't much matter whether the other twins knew he'd mentioned their names because he wouldn't be around for them to come after him for it.

Jimmy prodded him in the back to get him to go towards a doorway on the left. Tommy followed Sonny who was rather too enthusiastic about the surroundings.

"Fuck me, look at this place."

"Wait until you see downstairs," George said.

The twin led the way, Sonny going next, then Tommy and Jimmy behind. They went down a staircase with stone walls either side. At the bottom, a monitor on the left-hand wall. George and Sonny disappeared right, and Jimmy gave Tommy a shove. He stumbled forward into what he could only describe was a torture chamber. A spiked rack on the wall. Chains hanging from the ceiling above a trap door. Some mediaeval contraptions he'd only ever seen in books at school. A table with different tools on top, and at the far end, saws, one circular, the other more like a hedge cutter.

Ralph barked, drawing his attention, and Tommy stared into the corner at his mother sitting on the floor. She looked like she'd been crying, and he felt so guilty for telling her everything. All he'd done was hand his burden to her, and now she'd been dragged into…this. They made eye contact, and he wanted to tell her how sorry he was, but the audience prevented him from opening his mouth. It shouldn't, he should be prepared to apologise to her no matter how stupid it would make him feel with them all watching, because he had a strong feeling this was the last few minutes of his life.

"I'm sorry," she said. "I tried to help."

He smiled at her and nodded to show he didn't harbour any ill will, but the truth was he didn't trust himself to speak. He would look a right melon if he started crying, and it annoyed him that he was bothered by that, that it even mattered at this point. He'd likely be crying soon anyway from the pain of whatever George planned to do to him, so what difference did it make?

He took a deep breath and turned to George, defiant to the last. "So come on then, what the fuck am I supposed to have done?"

Chapter Thirty

Leaving France had been the best thing she'd ever done, and leaving Tommy was right up there as a second good decision. As soon as she'd woken up the next day after moving in with him, she'd noticed a change. His guard had shot up, he definitely wasn't the same man she'd gone to bed with, and something had told her to keep an eye on him and the way their relationship was going. With her ex, it had taken her far too long to see him for who he really was, and she'd promised herself when she'd left him that she'd never fall into the trap of being so reliant on another human being again.

She should have known Tommy seemed too good to be true, although maybe she was doing him a disservice. He'd been brilliant at first, online, and to have gone to the café to meet Mrs Blanchard and film a video of the place had been above and beyond. There had been times during the night, when she'd stared at the dark ceiling, when she'd asked herself if he'd designed it that way, to go to the café to make her think he'd do anything for her.

She'd gained an insight into his psyche while they'd chatted in private messages; it had become clear he had relationship issues. Trust issues. But she'd been prepared to be with him regardless. She'd made him well aware of what she felt about controlling men, so there would be no excuse in the future if he turned into one. She could even show him the messages she'd saved, to prove he'd condemned people who manipulated women—probably to lure her in so she thought he was one of the good guys.

In the end, she hadn't had to resort to that. When she'd announced she was leaving him, it was almost as if he was confused that she'd been the one to finish it and not him. But she'd warned him she was strong and independent and she didn't suffer fools gladly, so it shouldn't have been a surprise to him that she'd put her foot down early and refused to be moved around like a puppet.

When she'd got in the taxi, she'd seen him standing at the front door in her peripheral, and a part of her had wanted to turn around and wave, but not in a spiteful way, just a genuine goodbye, but with a man like Tommy, the gesture could have given him hope for the future, and while she didn't know him that well, or for that long, she knew him enough to know that leaving crumbs behind would be a huge mistake.

She'd settled into her flat above the café quickly, more so than she had at his house, which had always felt like it belonged to him and not her. She'd been an interloper there. The flat was hers and it contained her own furniture, the homeliness of her French residence here in London. She'd loved the grandeur of his house and all the mod cons—he even had a vacuum cleaner that worked all by itself while they were out at work—but she'd never felt at peace there, never truly comfortable, and now she understood why. It was Tommy, not the house, that had made her feel that way. It was Tommy who'd had her on edge.

Something inside had taken note of his behaviour and warned her he was not the one for her.

She'd settled into a routine. She got up early to bake the pastries, cakes, and baguettes, letting Harley in at around six when he came to add the fillings to the bread. After that, they had a break, drinking coffee and eating toast, and then Sally arrived to take over the front of house when it opened. She'd first been employed as a washer-upper but had swiftly shown she was a Jane of all trades. Harley left for his second job at around eight, and Leanora prepared the second batch of goodies.

Life had turned into something good, something happy, and the customers had welcomed her with open arms. There were now a few regulars she greeted by name each morning, and the only blot on her landscape was catching sight of Tommy sometimes. He stood on the other side of the road, probably thinking she hadn't seen him, but she had. He hadn't stayed for long, so she hadn't let it worry her, then he'd stopped coming altogether, unless he was hiding in the crowd or she was just too busy to glance outside these days and catch sight of him.

Another day was coming to an end, and she looked forward to having a bath and watching the television under a blanket on the sofa. There were still a fair few customers in, though, but if they left before the usual closing time, then Leanora would likely shut up shop early.

She sent Sally to her office to collect her wages. Leanora loaded up a tray that some customers had left on a table and took it out the back.

When she returned to stand behind the counter, there were no more customers. That was odd, because many of them had been halfway through their cake and coffee when she'd left them. In shock, and with the odd sense she'd walked into another dimension, she stared across at a man in a balaclava who stood on the other side of the counter with a shotgun pointed in her direction. Her heart rate kicked into high gear. Had he told everyone to get out?

She worried about Sally coming back to find this man here. Leanora looked away from him, through the glass in the door. One of her customers had fallen. She sat on the pavement, her skirt past her knees, scrapes on her skin.

"Close the blinds, there's a good girl," the man said. "I've already locked up, and if you were thinking of making a run for it out the back, I wouldn't bother because someone's out there with your little washing-up girl. Cute thing, isn't she."

Leanora's stomach flipped. She obeyed him, staring at a dribble of blood as it meandered down the customer's shin.

"I expect you want to know what I want," he said, "and it likely isn't what you think. Come and sit down with me and I'll explain."

She sat opposite him. What he said shit the life out of her. He sounded sincere when he said he'd kill her if she didn't do what he wanted.

"You're not going to be a snitch and tell the twins," he informed her. "In exchange for your cooperation, I won't kill you." He smiled. "I can't say fairer than that, can I?"

Chapter Thirty-One

George didn't appreciate being treated like a first-class prick, nor did he enjoy being smirked at, but he'd turn the tables soon enough and be the one smirking. He'd bide his time before he revealed his true intentions.

"You know exactly what you've done, but I can play your little game for a while. I warn you, though, that I get bored easily and my mood can change with the flick of a switch."

Tommy glanced from him to Greg and then behind George to Sonny and Jimmy who stood either side of the monitor. George hadn't expected those two to remain so had better make it clear their part in this was over.

"Thanks for your time, Jimmy, Sonny," George said. "It's best the pair of you fuck off.

"Thank God for that," Sonny muttered and legged it up the stairs.

Jimmy followed at a slower pace, and on the monitor, George watched them exit the building. Jimmy checked the door was shut behind them, then they got into the car and drove off.

George turned to face Tommy who stood in front of the chains.

"You might want to keep hold of your dog's collar," George said to Cheryl without looking her way. "I don't want him to get hurt." He smiled at Tommy. "Normally, we get people to strip naked to up the humiliation level, but seeing as your mother's got a front-row seat, I don't suppose she fancies seeing your knackers, so you can keep your boxer shorts on."

Tommy's cheeks flushed, and he shook his head as though in disbelief.

"Come on," George said. "Did you honestly think you wouldn't get in trouble for what you've done?"

"I caught Leanora selling drugs," Tommy said. "I saw a shitload of cocaine bricks in some boxes in her storeroom."

Cheryl shook her head—this wasn't the same story as hers.

"Which way did you enter the café?" George asked.

"The back," he said.

"Why did you go there?"

"I wanted to ask her if we could get back together. She let me in, and we were chatting in the storeroom, and like I said, I saw the bricks. I had a right go and told her she shouldn't have them on the premises and what the fuck was she thinking. She said she was selling them for some bloke and I ought to keep my nose out of it. I said I couldn't do that, I'd have to tell you, and she told me to get out. I saw red, and the next thing I knew, my hands were round her throat."

"Hands? Are you sure?"

"Yeah."

"No laces like you told your mum?"

"What?"

"And you expect us to believe you hurt Leanora out of the goodness of your heart—for our benefit?"

"Yeah, because that's what happened. I was well angry that she was selling drugs and you didn't know about it."

"So you killed her at the café, yes?"

"Yeah."

"I call bullshit on that, but whatever. So you strangled her. What happened next?"

Tommy told the rest of the story, and it resembled the one Leanora had told them, except he'd missed out the part where he'd taken her somewhere else to strangle her with the laces.

"She woke up in the woods, you know," George said. "Some old boy saw her, then he got hold of us. We went and picked her up. Then we went to see you." He didn't feel he had to add anything else.

"So why tell me she'd gone back to France when you knew she hadn't?"

"To see how you reacted. At first, I didn't think it was you, I thought the bloke in the clown mask was someone else, but then we thought about the van, and the mark on your face from the scissors, and the more we dug around, the more we discovered. And you told your poor fucking mother everything—what kind of son are you to put that on her? Look at her, she's shitting herself."

Tommy didn't glance her way, he was probably too ashamed, or maybe he didn't even give a shit, but Cheryl cried quietly, wiping tears and snot with the cuff of her sleeve. It was difficult to see her like that, especially when George imagined it as his own mother. There were lines you didn't cross, and dragging your mum into a mess like this was one of them.

"She apologised to you," George said, "but I didn't hear you do the same to her."

"I'm sorry," Tommy mumbled.

"Say it louder and like you mean it," Greg barked.

"I'm sorry."

Greg glared at him. "That's better. Now get undressed."

George nodded. "Yeah, I've had enough of playing games." He walked over to the tool table and selected a hammer, swinging it by his side as he returned to stand in front of Tommy who'd only just managed to take off his shoes. "Get a fucking move on, you moron."

Tommy stripped right down to his stripy boxer shorts and white socks.

"You can fucking get those off an' all." George pointed to the socks. "How am I supposed to cut your toes off with those on?"

Tommy hesitated a moment too long. George raised the hammer, went down in a quick crouch, and whacked Tommy's toes. Blood seeped through the sock, Tommy's scream echoing in the cellar, drowning out the faint rush of the Thames beneath him. George gave his foot another wallop and imagined the hammer making a dent in the top, the skin splitting. Tommy made the mistake of pushing George who fell backwards on his arse on the damp floor.

George stood, humiliation and anger burning through him. He advanced towards Tommy who limped away in reverse with his hands held up.

"It's too late to call a truce now," George said, raising the hammer and bringing it round in an arc until the claw end disappeared into Tommy's cheek.

It met with resistance where it had smacked into his teeth, his gums, and rather than pull the claw out gently, George wrenched it so the skin ripped. Blood pissed everywhere, down to the jaw and the neck to soak into Tommy's jacket collar. Cheryl sobbed in the corner, the sound of her despair drowned out by her son's screeching.

"Keep the noise down, you fucking fanny," George said to him.

He nodded to Greg who came over to help drag Tommy onto the trapdoor. George dropped the hammer deliberately on Tommy's other foot, and together they attached the manacles to his wrists. George went over to the contraption on the wall and turned the handle. The chains shortened until Tommy hung about a foot off the floor. George bent down to rip his socks off so he could inspect the damage. Unhappy with what he saw, he went to the tool table and collected some cigar cutters. Back with Tommy, he crouched and held the injured foot, digging his thumb into the circular, bleeding dent. He positioned the cutters over the little toe and glanced up at the hanging man.

"This is going to sting," George said and at the same time squeezed the cutter handles together.

The toe dropped onto the trapdoor, blood dripping from the gash left behind. George pushed his finger into the dent even harder and finished the job of chopping off all the toes. Tommy's wailing ceased; he fainted. Now that George's suit was ruined by the damp floor and the blood, it'd be burned later on. There was no need to put on a forensic suit now, but he cursed himself for not putting one on earlier. He stared at the bleeding foot to the sound of Cheryl keening. He could be cruel and check whether she had her eyes close and force her to open them, to watch, but he was feeling oddly benevolent and would let her shut everything out if she had to.

While they waited for Tommy to come round, George went upstairs and made everyone a coffee, going back down to pass one to Cheryl who seemed surprised at being given something to drink.

"I'd give you popcorn for the rest of the show, but we haven't got any." George laughed and leaned against the wall, staring at Tommy and contemplating what else he could do once the little bastard woke up.

Carving YOU CUNT into Tommy's stomach with a Stanley knife was one of the most satisfying things George had ever done while someone was out for the count. He usually did this sort of thing when they were awake, and the jostling of them trying to get away from the blade tended to mess things up. He used his suit jacket sleeve to wipe the blood away, then turned Tommy on the chains towards his mother so she could see what had been written.

"No one's going to see that except for us, though," he said, "because I'll be chopping him up into pieces later on."

Cheryl scrunched her eyes shut and screamed, her dog howling beside her.

George had had enough of waiting. He went upstairs to collect some water in a bucket and came down to throw it on Tommy's face. It didn't have the desired effect of waking him up, so George took a moment to check whether the bloke had a pulse. He did, and it was quite strong, considering.

"Are you hungry?" George asked Greg.

"I could do with a curry."

"What sort do you want, Cheryl?" George didn't expect her to take him up on the offer, she probably felt sick, food the last thing on her mind, but he was nothing if not polite.

"I don't want anything," she said then tacked on a thank you as though she'd realised she'd sounded rude.

"He could be out a fair while, so if you want to get some kip, be my guest." George jerked his head at her so she followed him. He led the way upstairs, glancing over his shoulder to find she was behind him and Greg was behind her, the dog taking up the rear. "We've got some mattresses in that cupboard over there for when we need to sleep over, and we've not long had a sofa bed delivered, and that telly. Sometimes we have our blokes babysit people, and they like to have a go on the PlayStation."

Although a lot of the babysitting was done at the cottage now, then when it came time to kill, they brought the bodies here. The smell from the dead beneath the steel room had finally gone away.

"Would you like a mattress and a blanket, Cheryl?" George asked.

Surprisingly, she nodded. Maybe she thought going to sleep was the best bet so she could block everything out for a while. The carving on

Tommy's stomach and the wounds on his feet would only drip small amounts of blood, George wasn't worried about him dying from the loss, so they'd leave the little bastard hanging down there until after they'd eaten their dinner.

George sent a message to Moody who had stopped his surveillance at Tommy's house earlier and taken the lifted fingerprints to the private detective who'd matched them to Tommy. George would tell mother and son all about that later if he had the chance, but for now, he put a food order through to Moody and asked him to buy a meal for himself, too, and bring it all here. Just in case Cheryl changed her mind, he picked a korma and pilau rice for her.

He sorted her a mattress, the thin wipe-over kind the police used in cells. She lay on the floor with the dog beside her, the blanket over them both. George felt sorry for her really, grassing on her son, thinking they'd go easy on him when it had been anything but so far. She had to understand, though, that when residents misbehaved they had to be punished, regardless of how their mothers felt about it. Yes, he was giving her nightmare fodder for the rest of her life, but what was the alternative? Could he pretend he believed his story and banish Tommy from London instead of killing him? George had to remember it wasn't just his decision to make. In the past he'd gone ahead and done things anyway, then Greg had a go at him afterwards.

When he thought Cheryl was asleep, he went and sat beside his brother at the long table. "I feel a bit sorry for that poor cow. Shall we make him leave London and that can be the end of it?"

Greg stared at him. "Are you taking the piss? He thought he'd killed Leanora. This bollocks about him doing it for our benefit is just that, bollocks. He's trying to pull the wool over your eyes, and I'd have thought you of all people would have seen that."

"Fair enough, I was just bothered about his mother and how she's going to cope with this going forward."

"If you're that bothered about how upset she's going to be and what state her mental health will be in, fucking kill her as well, and then she won't have to think, will she."

George frowned at Greg's unusual display of arseholeness. "That isn't like you."

"Remember, she was only sorry once she realised we knew Leanora was alive and what had happened to her. She was prepared to lie for her boy until then, so that makes her complicit. Then she told us what he'd told her to say, that he'd only done it because he feared being poor. I mean, what? I think you'd be a dick to let her walk away from this without at least giving her a Cheshire."

"But if I slice her face, her neighbours are going to know it was me, and then it'll bring attention to the fact that Tommy's gone 'missing'. They'll guess he isn't missing and that I killed him. Do we want the pigs sniffing around regarding that?"

Greg shrugged. "Break her fucking legs instead then."

For some reason, George didn't want to hurt Cheryl. "I'm going to banish her. She can sod off out of London. That way I haven't got to feel guilty when I see her, and if she ends up killing herself over this then we'll never hear about it."

"I don't trust her enough for you to do that," Greg said. "This is a woman prepared to bullshit us for her son. She's going to want justice for us killing him. She's the sort to come back years later and stab us in the back—literally."

George sighed. "Then *you* kill her."

"And the dog?"

"We're not killing Ralph. He can be our new best friend. We'll get him to a vet so any chip he's got can be replaced so *we're* down as his new owners, not her."

Greg smiled.

Chapter Thirty-Two

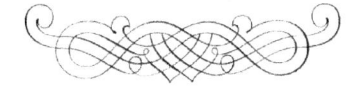

Leanora never thought she'd want to see someone dying, but when Will had received a message asking him to see if she wanted to watch Tommy 'meet his maker', she'd found herself agreeing. Why? The burning rage festering inside her—he'd tried to kill her, twice; he'd dumped her in the woods; then he'd apparently gone back there this morning. To what, visit the scene of the crime and gloat? She'd known he was a controlling, nasty piece-of-work *raton* but she'd never imagined he'd murder her.

The journey to wherever he was had been made in silence—she didn't know what she'd have said to Will anyway. Having a blindfold on was unnerving, and she'd had to concentrate on her breathing to take her mind off the fact her eyes were covered.

Anxiety kicked in. *Would* she be able to stand there and watch someone die? Would it depend on the method of murder? Blood, and lots of it, might ensure she turned away. Violence…

The car came to a stop, and her stomach rolled over.

Will gently clasped her wrist. "I'll come round to your side and guide you out. Sorry about all this subterfuge, but this new place…it's got recognisable landmarks across the river, and the twins won't want you knowing where they conduct this side of their business."

She nodded—if she didn't know where she was, she couldn't put them in the shit if she was asked by the police later down the line, could she. Christ, what if the authorities got involved? What if Tommy was reported missing and they looked into it? Would they poke into the fact she'd had some post sent to his house once upon a time? He'd been so angry about that, as if he didn't want anyone to know she'd officially lived there.

She waited for Will to exit then help her out. Cold air wrapped around her. She held his hand as he walked her along, then told her to stop. A gust of warmth hit her, as did the smell of curry, then she was aided inside. The click of a door shutting, then the blindfold came off. She glanced around to get her bearings. Greg stood with a woman and a dog. George beside a man she didn't recognise.

"This is Tommy's mother," George said. "Cheryl. She'll be watching the proceedings, too. And this is Mr Moody, one of our men. He'll be off in a sec, though. He's been working hard today collecting evidence and whatnot."

She knew who Moody was now. The man who'd come to the safe house to collect the café keys so he could pick up the empty cardboard boxes. He'd returned the keys to Will later on, but she hadn't seen him.

She nodded a hello to both people—it felt weird to do that to Tommy's mother, strange that their first meeting should be on the day he died, not the day she'd come to London to live with him.

Greg let Moody and Will out, then he rolled up a mattress on the floor and put it and a blanket in a cupboard. Someone must have been asleep down there. She glanced at Cheryl—it looked likely it was her, face creased on one side, her hair sticking up.

Where was Tommy?

What would it feel like to see him again?

"We'll fuck off downstairs now then," George said.

He led the way. Greg gave Cheryl a gentle push. She and the dog followed George. Leanora remained in place, stuck there, telling herself to move forward but unable to. Everything in her had frozen.

"If you've changed your mind, then go and sit at the table and wait," Greg said. "It's not unusual to get cold feet when it comes down to it."

Leanora shook her head. "I need to at least see him. Not necessarily watch him die, though."

Greg nodded. "I understand."

At last she moved and followed him down some claustrophobic stairs; the walls went down either side, giving a narrow tunnel effect, blocking off whatever lay at the bottom to the right. She turned into a cellar-type room, the stone of the walls mouldy in places and sweating with damp in the corners. Halogen heaters and lamps at the edges lit up the centre, a trapdoor in the floor, Tommy hanging above it from chains in just his boxer shorts. His chin touched his chest, his eyes closed where he was either asleep or unconscious. She imagined the latter, considering he had no toes on one foot and a horrible dent in the top. She frowned at the words on Tommy's torso.

YOU CUNT.

She couldn't disagree with it, but the pain that must have come with the letters being carved would have been immense. She'd loved this man once—or she'd thought she had—and to see him like this, as a vulnerable person, eclipsed her feelings of hatred that he was the man in the clown mask. Only for a moment, though, because the reminder of that mask brought back all the nasty feelings.

The pain must have been too much for him to stay awake.

Good.

What kind of person had she become to think that way? To be glad he'd been hurting?

When someone's killing you, you tend to hate them.

George wafted something beneath Tommy's nose which did the trick in waking him up. Tommy lifted his head, his eyes seeming to creak open in increments as though the lids were too heavy. He frowned at Leanora, and it was obvious he thought he might be dreaming—she hadn't been here when he'd fallen asleep, so how the hell could she be here now? Maybe he wasn't thinking straight, his mind hadn't got to the part where it told him she could have been brought to wherever they were. He must be groggy from the agony of torture.

"So you're not in France then," he rasped.

She didn't bother saying no because it was obvious.

"What did you do, tell them all about me?" he asked. "Get them to play with my head, coming round to my gaff and telling me you'd gone missing? Was it funny to play mind games? Get me back? Well, you can fuck off, you stupid Frog slag."

She glanced at his mother who stared at her son as if she didn't know him anymore, confused as to how he could speak to Leanora with such spite in his tone.

"He was like this a lot near the end of our relationship," Leanora said to her. "Women are beneath him. I lost count of the times he spoke to me like I was a piece of shit. So I left him. His response was to murder me. Why? Because I was going to let the twins know what was happening in my storeroom and at my back door in the middle of the night. I had the audacity to want him and his two friends out of my life."

"I'm so sorry," Cheryl said. "I had no idea he was capable of the things he's done. I thought he was… I thought he was a good man. I brought him up to be one, and it went wrong somewhere."

Leanora smiled at her. "I wish I could have met you under different circumstances."

Cheryl nodded then reached down to stroke the dog's head. Did she need the comfort from the feel of the fur? She lowered herself to the floor beside him, and he flopped onto her lap.

Leanora returned her attention to Tommy. "Who are Numbers One and Two?"

He narrowed his eyes. "What the fuck are you talking about?"

"The men in the balaclavas, who are they?"

His laugh echoed. "Oh, them. They're no one you need to know about."

George stepped forward and pressed a gloved fingertip into one of the slices in Tommy's chest. "But I do. Your mum never said anything about them, so either you didn't tell her or it's one bit of info she's not aware of."

Tommy winced but held it together well. "I didn't tell her. And you're not going to get me to grass them up. They're just people paid to do a job. Nothing more."

"We'll find out who they are eventually," George said. "We're good at poking into people's lives, picking out acquaintances. When we find them, we'll let them know it was you who sent us their way."

Tommy bristled. "But it wasn't."

George smiled. "You're not exactly going to be in a position to stop us, though, are you? You're going to be chopped up in bits."

It seemed Tommy had only just realised he was *actually* going to die. He must have known it on some other level but had perhaps convinced himself that he could get out of this, that even though the twins were known for being monstrous, they wouldn't kill a son in front of his mother. He'd maybe latched on to the hope that he'd lose more toes and maybe his fingers, he'd suffer more torture but he'd be banished from London instead of removed from it permanently.

Even Leanora could see, from the look on George's face, that Tommy would never make it out of here alive. And she was okay with that. Rewind her life a few hours and she was being murdered. Tommy hadn't cared beyond the fact that he needed her gone. He needed her shut up for good. He'd have continued his life without a care in the world had he not been caught.

"I bet you're sick to your stomach that I didn't die," she said, enjoying the way her words had landed.

He gritted his teeth.

"You couldn't even get a simple strangulation right," she said. "Oh, and the botched suffocation."

"Oh God." Cheryl whimpered.

"I'm going to go to therapy with a man called Vic who's going to fix everything broken inside my mind—everything *you* broke." Leanora took a deep breath. "And I'm going to move on from this, I'm going to stay in the café, and I'll open another one day, realise my dreams despite you wanting to snuff them out. To snuff me out. You're nothing spectacular, Tommy, no matter how many times you've told yourself you are. Because look at you, you're hanging from chains, you're about to be killed, and only your mother is going to give a shit about it."

She turned away from him and walked up the stairs, going to sit at the table. She'd likely hear him screaming soon, but she could poke her fingers in her ears to deaden the sound, then she could go back home to her flat, leaving this blip in the road behind her.

Because that's all she'd allow him to be now. A blip.

Chapter Thirty-Three

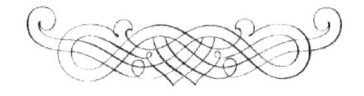

Now that Leanora had buggered off, George could get into the swing of things. "Greg, make a note that after we've got rid of this geezer, we'll get the ball rolling on finding his accomplices."

"Why wait? I'll get the private detective on it now." Greg took the work phone from George and got on with sending a message.

George looked at Tommy to gauge what the bloke was thinking. He appeared smug; he thought they wouldn't find the balaclava men. In truth, they probably wouldn't. Because the men had their faces covered, if Bennett scoured the CCTV for them out the front of the café, there would be sod all features to see. Unless people talked, then they may come to a dead end with regards to Tommy's cohorts.

"Before you ask," Cheryl said, "I swear I don't know who they are."

George studied her. "Get the PI to start with our new best friend at the car showroom." He stared at their captive.

Tommy gave the exact reaction George was after. He jolted, looking to the ceiling in thought, then he made eye contact with George. "*My* showroom?"

"What other one is there?"

"You said 'our new best friend'."

George nodded and smiled. "The manager you've employed is a lovely fella. Lionel. He drove your van all the way to a designated spot so our man could test the back of it. Did you know that even if you think you've cleaned something properly with bleach, you most likely haven't? DNA was found, and it's in the process of being tested to see if it's a match for Leanora's. There are fingerprints. You really should have bagged her hands when you transported her if you had no intention of torching or getting the van disposed of. Also, your fingerprints were found on the empty boxes in the café storeroom. I think this proves you're the man in the clown mask, but then our Mr Moody confirmed that when he found the mask at your place—as well as Leanora's phone."

Tommy clamped his mouth shut.

"Got nothing to say?" George taunted. "What provisions have you got in place when you die, or hadn't you got around to sorting that out yet?"

"What do you mean?"

"Who gets your house? Your business?"

"My mum. I made a will last year."

Tommy shut his eyes and hung his head back, blowing out a deep breath, his bottom lip wobbling. This was getting to him then. He was properly realising this was the end of his road.

George stepped forward and whipped out the Stanley knife from his pocket. He flipped the button so the blade popped out, then raked it down Tommy's stomach. He hacked and hacked, obliterating the words, making a complete mess. Tommy screeched. Frustrated he wasn't getting the desired effect (the blade was too short), George moved to the tool table, dropping the Stanley knife in a bucket of soapy bleach water, then selected a machete with a blade of about ten inches.

Cheryl let out a short, sharp scream.

George ignored her, advancing towards Tommy and plunging the steel into the point just below the rib cage. He carved deep, creating a circle, and as the round of skin flopped forward, the intestines followed. They dangled over Tommy's wedding tackle, blood pissing everywhere. Cheryl shuffled around on her backside so she faced the wall, and George gave his brother a nod then held up a finger to ask him to wait a sec.

George reached up to clasp a screaming Tommy by the arm, turning him on the chains to face his mother. He nodded to Greg again who produced a gun and fired into the back of

Cheryl's head. The dog yelped in fright and skittered away, blood spatter on his fur. He darted up the stairs. Tommy's scream wasn't only for himself now. It sounded full of his anger, helplessness, and possibly regret. George sliced his throat to shut the motherfucker up, then stepped back to watch him bleed out.

Greg unravelled their recently installed hosepipe and drenched the wall to get rid of Cheryl's blood and brain matter that had landed there. He came to stand beside George and hosed Tommy down.

With two bodies to saw up, there was plenty of work to do.

Better get to it then.

Chapter Thirty-Four

Noel was so annoyed. Why the fuck wasn't Tommy answering his messages? The buyers had come and gone, taking the last of the drugs. Noel wanted to arrange where to drop Tommy's money off so this job could be finished once and for all—and their association with him—but it seemed Tommy wasn't bothered about responding. His need to break their alliance clearly wasn't as strong as Noel's. The bastard was probably fast asleep, considering he thought they'd be leaving the cash in his compost bin.

"I'm going to ring him," Noel said to his brother as they drove away from the location where they'd left the buyers. "And if he doesn't answer me, then we'll keep all the money, not just the portion he told us to pay ourselves."

"Yeah, that can be the penalty for him not answering in time."

Noel pressed Tommy's number and listen to the ringing in his ear. Then it stopped. "About fucking time. What the hell have you been doing that means you haven't been responding to me?"

"Tommy's dead," a man said—a recognisable voice. "So is his mother. That's what happens when you do things and The Brothers find out. I take it I'm speaking to one of the gentlemen who does little jobs for Tommy."

A nasty spike of dread went through Noel. Fuck, their name would come up on Tommy's phone screen. What was it he'd saved them as? NoJo? This fucker might work out who they were from that.

Noel stabbed at the screen to end the call, shitting himself. "Fucking hell, fucking hell, fucking hell…"

"What's happened?" Joel indicated to park at the side of the street.

"Don't stop! Keep bloody going." Noel turned the burner phone off, wiped it over with the sleeve of his coat, then lobbed it out of the window so it landed in shrubbery.

"What the fuck's going on?" Joel kept driving.

Noel closed the window and blew out a long breath. "I think I've just spoken to George."

"What? *The* George?"

"Yeah. He said Tommy and his mum are dead. He asked if I'm one of the people who works with Tommy. Jesus Christ, do you think they know who we are?"

Joel whistled, a long note that seemed to go on forever. "Shit. Okay, let's think about this for a second. No panicking. If Tom and Cheryl are dead, it means Tommy's been caught for killing Leanora, right?"

"George mentioning me being one of the people Tommy works with… It can only mean Tommy's *said* he works with people."

"If he didn't use your name, then I'd say Tommy and Cheryl kept their mouths shut."

"But what if they didn't and George is messing with my head? The twins will come after us."

"But we've always thought they might. We've always lived with the worry they'd cotton on to who was impersonating them on their Estate—if they even know about it. It's time to stop doing that. Keep our noses clean on that score."

Noel nodded. It was true, they'd always skated close to the wind by pretending to be the twins. If this wasn't a warning for them to pack it in now, he didn't know what was. And if they didn't listen and things went completely tits up, then they only had themselves to blame.

"We'll have a sit-down and work out where we go from here," Noel said.

Joel nodded. "We might need to revamp our business model."

That's an understatement.

Chapter Thirty-Five

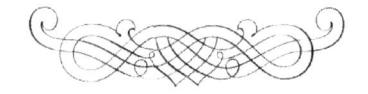

Knackered and in no mood to work any longer, considering it was the early hours of the morning, George turned to his brother, who was driving them home. "I bet you any money if a check is run on that phone number, it'll come to a dead end."

Greg nodded. "Of course it will. People who deal in drugs have got untold amounts of burners on the go. Whoever it was you just spoke to has probably disposed of it already. You're going to have to accept that we might not be able to find them, whoever this NoJo is."

"I should have pushed Tommy and Cheryl to tell us who they were. I knew damn well they wore balaclavas and one of them waved a shotgun around, so it's not as if I wasn't aware they're dangerous people."

"It was obvious they weren't going to give up their real names, so don't beat yourself up about it."

George would take that advice, too tired to ponder any further. Their identity would always bug him, unless they found Tommy's little helpers, but with him no longer in the equation, he wouldn't be able to ask them to do any more work for him, would he.

But they're likely the type to do that sort of job anyway, using weapons, scaring people. A bit like us. Tommy being gone won't stop them.

"What are we going to call the dog?" George asked.

"He's used to being called Ralph. Best not confuse him, eh?"

"Fair enough. Where's he going to sleep? We haven't got a bed for him."

"We'll sort something when we get home."

George frowned. "Do you reckon he's going to miss Cheryl?"

"Of course he is."

"There's going to be times we can't take him with us. What do we do then?"

"Fucking hell, bruv, how do you think other people who've got dogs cope? They go to work and leave them at home. We'll get him a load of toys to keep him occupied, maybe one of those big crates."

George took his phone out to investigate how to care for a dog and called into the back of the van, "You'll be all right with us, mate. We'll look after you."

Ralph poked his head between the front seats and licked George's cheek.

Shit, I'm going to get attached.

"Pack that in," George said, going for stern. "We don't do kisses, right?"

Ralph retreated.

"Meany head," Greg muttered.

"Piss off." But George *did* feel bad.

Bollocks.

Chapter Thirty-Six

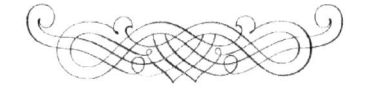

A week or so after the van argument, this Saturday was coming to an end with Sandra's younger kids much more content with fuller bellies, and they'd fallen asleep easily. It amazed her that even though she'd sworn she'd shielded them from her money worries to some degree, now they knew she wouldn't be so skint with her 'new job from home', they'd relaxed.

Sandra and Sally finally sat on the sofa with a cup of tea. Sandra was that knackered she hadn't even bothered closing the curtains. They'd been blowing up balloons and getting the living room decorated for the youngest's birthday tomorrow. The telly played in the background, but neither of them watched it. They stared outside instead.

Despite it being dark, she could see several people entering the house opposite, the orange light from the lamppost showing their silhouettes.

"What the fuck's going on there?" Sandra got up and moved to the window. "There's a car. Probably a taxi. Jerry must be having one of his parties."

"Bloody hell." Sally yawned. "I'm going to bed now then before he cranks the music up."

"All right, love." Sandra shut the curtains, thinking she'd do the same.

Chapter Thirty-Seven

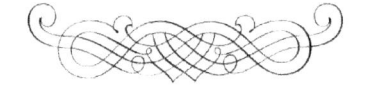

Empress stood in the living room and wondered how the fuck she'd got there. Well, she knew how, of course she bloody did, but she hadn't expected this job to turn out the way it had. What was supposed to be her poking into the strange practise of women lying on large stones in the middle of nowhere, pretending to be sacrifices, had turned into her and another three women being carted from house to house every evening to service certain residents of the Cardigan Estate.

She really needed to get to the toilet so she could use her phone. Julian, one of the two men who lived with her and the women in the house with the boarded-up windows, didn't know she had a burner. She'd been with them long enough for him to trust her anyway, so there was no way he'd imagine she owned one. She hid it in a special pouch inside her knickers and only ever switched it on when she needed to use it. Her *real* boss didn't know the half of what went on, because how could she tell a detective inspector that she'd gone so far undercover that she was involved in sex with strangers?

Fuck knows how this is going to work out when it goes to court, if it even does.

She'd probably get raked over the coals and find herself in a heap of trouble with her senior officers, but for now, she was doing what was necessary to catch the big boss of this operation—the High Priest.

The sacrificial rituals had creeped her out the first time she'd participated, all those men standing around, watching, chanting. She'd reported to the DI what had gone on, but as she was unable to tell him where the stones were—they were blindfolded on the journey—or get out of the house to escape, she was kind of stuck.

Until now.

She let Julian know she needed the loo and went upstairs. Sitting on the toilet, she sent a message.

DS LITTLE: I'M AT A HOUSE. MANAGED TO PEEK UNDER MY BLINDFOLD. FOUR ALDING CLOSE. WHAT DO YOU WANT ME TO DO?

DI TAYLOR: STAY PUT. WE'LL BE WITH YOU SHORTLY. WHO'S THERE?

DS LITTLE: RESIDENT—A MALE CALLED JERRY. ME, THE THREE OTHER WOMEN, AND JULIAN.

DI TAYLOR: SEE YOU SOON.

She turned the phone off and put it back inside her knickers. If tonight went like it usually did, they'd tease Jerry for a while then go upstairs to do the business. Empress had become a different person, immersing herself in this role, and in a way she was sad it was coming to an end. She'd wanted to find this High Priest, arrest him, but it seemed DI Taylor was calling it a day. She couldn't blame him, this operation had been going on for long enough with zero results.

She was going to have to accept that some cases didn't get solved.

Unless she blew the whole thing. Julian would *really* trust her then, and maybe he'd take her into his confidence a bit more. She'd worked too hard on this to let it all go now.

Taylor was going to give her hell when he found out what she was about to do.

If he found out.

She went down to the living room and gave Julian a panicked look.

He joined her out in the hallway. "What's the matter?"

"Blue lights through the bathroom window."

"Fuck. They might not be coming here, though."

"Do you want to stick around and find out?"

He glanced into the living room at Jerry who had the three women on their knees around him. "Jesus wept. Girls, we need to get a shift on."

Jerry frowned. "Hang on a bloody minute, I've paid for an hour!"

"Coppers are on the way," Julian said. "We'll leave out the back."

He gestured for the women to follow him, but Fantasy ran towards the front door instead. Julian hesitated, clearly working out whether he could afford to let her go or not. He shrugged and gripped the wrists of the other two, Empress following behind them, out through a side door in the kitchen and down to a gate at the bottom of the garden. As they hustled down a dark alley at the rear of the houses, the flash of blue lights from the front lit up the sky.

"Run!" Empress whisper-shouted. "Fucking run!"

To be continued in *Regal*,
the Cardigan Estate 39

Printed in Great Britain
by Amazon